THE CARNIVAL'S SECRET

Zachary Hogarth

Contents

CHAPTER 1

I have cleaned the main bedroom, guest bedroom, kitchen, and living room, practically the whole house. And now, just as I am about to finish, she wants me to leave what I am currently working on, the dining room, and clean her pool house. The old lady doesn't even use the pool house.

Ms. Betty has always been an odd one when it came to cleaning her house. I have worked for the seventy-four-year-old woman for about six months, and she still likes throwing curveballs at me.

She writes on the schedule every week what she wants me to clean, and I plan on cleaning it, but when I start to do it, she stops me and tells me she needs me somewhere else. The old lady is lovely and all, but she is definitely not organized, and she should not be making the schedule.

One would think that since the old lady makes such a mess of the schedule, she would have a messy house, but that is untrue. Ms. Betty is one of the cleanest people in town. Every time I go over to clean her house, there are almost no specks of dirt or dust. It is so spotless that I think she does a little cleaning or something before I come over, which defeats the whole purpose of my house cleaning job.

I rush to clean the pool house while still being as thorough as possible. The pool house is beach-themed, so everything is either white or light blue, which makes seeing dirt and dust easier. I start with the vacuum, then mop the floors. After that, I work on cleaning the bathroom, and then I go to work on the small decorative table set she has just for the pool house. Yes, she has a particular table set for her pool house and a more extensive and fancier table set for her main house since one is just not enough apparently.

Once I am finished with the whole pool house, it is almost three o'clock. My work here is done for the day, so I run out of Ms. Betty's house before she can catch me. Ms.Betty is known for her talking. I usually don't have a problem listening to her crazy rants and stories, but today is different. Today I promised my brother Devin I wouldn't be home late.

I quickly walk down the smooth paved road of the town until it turns to dirt. My family's house sits hidden deep in the trees. My great-grandfather built it many years ago and said it was the best work he had ever done.

The house is made of wood and stone. The wooden front door has unique carvings of lines that are so fluent and intricate that it looks like it should be in a museum. The inside of the house contains many rooms, each one with its own handcrafted wooden archway. The house is impressive, and I know I will be disappointed when I move out of it one day.

My great-grandfather helped build and design many of the houses in our town when it was first built fifty years after the war ended. The government of the New World wanted some good to emerge from the bad and decided to construct beautiful towns over the ruins of the old battlefields where many people died. In the end, eighteen towns were built over the most memorable spots.

In the beginning, not much of a battle went on where our town Treegrass is. According to my old history teacher, the event that occurred in this area was primarily a stalemate.

For ten years, men hid behind their walls and trenches, only sometimes shooting at each other until one day, the people of the New World decided to stop hiding and start fighting. All the men agreed to attack at the same time. This took the enemy by surprise and we won, but not without losing many good men.

At the war's end, the government took down the walls that the troops on both sides used to defend themselves and leveled the area to a blank slate. From there, they brought in people to design and make a place for people to live peacefully, my great-grandfather being one of them. Not only did he build our house and some others, but he was also asked to help build the town center, which was a big honor.

After all the buildings were made, trees and plants started to grow fast, so the government decided to name our town Treegrass, creative I know. It's known as a place for people to grow and thrive, or at least that is what's on the news each day when they talk about what's going on in all the towns.

My brother Devin and I love watching the news most days to see what it's like in other towns since visiting another town is not likely for us. The people always look so happy. I have always wanted to visit another town just to see if it really looks as great as it does on the TV.

The people on the TV are always smiling, laughing, and having a good time. It sometimes makes me wonder if people in other towns see Treegrass the same way we see them. We are pretty happy here in Treegrass so I imagine that our faces reflect the ones we see on the news. The only time they show anything else on the news is if they are discussing the war, or if there is another storm coming.

Since there are a few towns located along the coast, things like hurricanes are a common topic. There is an average of at least one hurricane hitting Treegrass a year, but we have become accustomed to this reality. I have grown to like the way the sky would darken, and the rain would pound on the roof. If the storms weren't so destructive, then I would wish for a hurricane more often.

Since the towns are not built close to one another, it is too dangerous for just anyone to travel to another town. The only time they allow this is if you have connections in other towns or if you are very smart and the government decides you can be of use in another town. If that happens, then you would be transported in a car to get wherever you are going. Cars are a rare sight around here, so this never goes unnoticed.

Over time, Devin and I made up a game where we both try to predict what the news is going to be about before the news anchor tells us. It is only early spring, so we both know there wont be a hurricane for a while, but other storms aren't out of the question.

Yesterday, the town to the far north of us got snow, and the news showed people outside standing around the news anchor waiting for her to talk. Each person has specks of snow on their clothes and bright red cheeks. Devin guessed they were having snowball fights, while I guessed they were sledding.

Devin was right this time, as the reporter then told the story of how the kids got let out of school early so they could play and have snowball fights. They showed videos of the kids hiding behind snow forts and running from their friends who held the snowballs.

Games like these keep the two of us occupied most of the time, but today is different. Today is the day that they're bringing in the carnival. Devin and I first saw the advertisement for it two weeks ago, and we couldn't stop thinking about it since. It showed people of all ages playing so many different kinds of games and eating food that we have never seen before.

Devin and I have always had a love of playing games. We like to have friendly competitions so naturally the thought of a place that contains so many games excited us, especially since we have never seen most of the games they showed in the advertisement.

We both ran to our parents to tell them about it. Our Dad promised to take us, which was not surprising since he always encouraged us to create our own games so we could challenge ourselves. Our Dad has always been very adventurous and understanding.

Our Mom, on the other hand, is more introverted and cautious about new things. It is amazing how two completely different people fell for one another. When asked if she wanted to go to the carnival, she unsurprisingly said no.

Our Mom will probably stay home and make the colorful blankets that she likes to sell on the weekends. A lot of townspeople love walking by her little stand and looking at the detailed blankets. Some buy them just so they can hang them up in their homes.

I walk through the front door of our house and I am immediately greeted by my dog Mud.

"Hey boy, where's Dad?" I ask Mud.

"In here," I hear from the kitchen. I make my way over to see him already making our early dinner for today. Devin wanted us to eat early before going to the carnival tonight. He has been so excited to go and thinks he will miss it if we aren't out the door by four o'clock.

"Excited? I know Devin is. I just know he will be talking about this carnival for months after it has left," my Dad says. I can't help but agree.

"Months? I think we are still going to hear about it years from now. This carnival is the first source of real entertainment this town has ever seen," I tell my Dad.

It's true, aside from very small school gatherings, there has been nothing else to do around here besides work or school. This has made people so bored that whenever something new comes to town, everybody knows about it and tries to get as involved with it as possible until that too gets boring.

Dad laughs and continues cooking. Mom walks in from working at the flower shop down the street. Her hair lays loose in a bun on top of her hair, and her glasses rest on her bright pink shirt. She comes into the kitchen, having seemed to have forgotten what today was. Then she looks up as if realizing.

"The carnival is here already. I thought that wasn't for another week?"

"No, Mom, it is today. It is not too late to change your mind and join us you know," I tell her, but I know she wouldn't. My Mother just mumbles a response, and my Dad states that dinner is ready.

Within seconds I hear my younger brother come running down the stairs and into the kitchen. He takes his seat at the table with a giant smile on his face.

"Hey Sam, are you ready for the carnival tonight?" He says with the biggest smile on his face. I nod knowing he is much more excited about going than I am. He has probably been thinking about this all day in school while I worked.

Don't get me wrong, I'm excited to go and play games, but Devin has more energy than me since he's only sixteen. I think that I have lost some of my energy since I graduated from school and started cleaning houses.

I nod happily in response and begin eating. Devin starts talking about what he thinks the carnival will be like, and my parents and I can't help but smile and laugh at his enthusiasm.

Devin has always been the more free-spirited and outspoken one, while I usually like to keep more to myself. I think that Devin is treating this carnival as one of the last times to have fun before he has to find a job when he turns eighteen like I did.

My father did construction when he turned eighteen because his father ran the business. He worked there up until he retired two years ago. Unlike my Dad, my Mother changed her job multiple times before deciding that she liked the flower shop the best. She can work there on the weekdays and still have time to make her blankets to sell on the weekends for some extra cash.

When four o'clock comes around, Devin is rushing us out the door, and my Mom sits outside on the deck working on one of her latest blankets. The blanket she is working on now looks to be a design I have seen a few times before. It is a series of blues, each shade of blue fades into another shade of blue that is either lighter or darker, but all the blues are formatted in a way that creates different shapes. She waves us goodbye with Mud sitting by her side.

The carnival was put up on the far south side of our town, and since we live not too far from there, we decide to walk instead of taking our bikes. They have been working to put the carnival up for two days now, and Devin and I haven't gotten a chance to sneak a peek at what the carnival will look like. All we know is what the advertisement said.

As we approached the colorful lights and giant walls of curtains, we begin to hear music. Bikes that people rode on to get here line the outside of the carnival. There is a line of people waiting to get in, but it moves fast.

There is a man at the entrance who is dressed in a gray and black uniform and has two other people in uniform at his side. These men are standing straighter, reminding me of a more serious version of the school security guards.

When it becomes Devin's turn, the man at the entrance inserts a card into a machine and then asks for his name and age. After that, he does some typing on the machine, and then the card pops back out a second later. He hands Devin the card.

"What's that for?" My Dad asks, and I wonder the same thing.

The man replies, "You will need this card for any game that you wish to play. I have printed your name and age on it so it does not get mixed up with someone else's."

We all nod in understanding, and then it is my turn. "Samantha Ivory, age eighteen," I tell the man. He writes this down and moves on to my Dad. Once we all have our cards, we are finally able to walk into the carnival and take it all in.

Chapter 2

The colorful lights of the carnival make it appear as though I just walked into some sort of dreamland. I look around at everything in front of me, but it's hard to focus on just one thing.

There are games everywhere.

To my right, there is a row of people sitting down, pointing guns that shoot water into the mouths of fake shark heads. As the one shark's head rises above the others quicker, people start cheering, and a few seconds later a bell is rung. Everyone gets up to leave, and a woman gives the winning kid a piece of candy. I like this place already.

To my left, people are standing around watching two people holding onto a bar above their heads, their feet not touching the ground. I don't understand the game, but people seem to be having a good time watching.

There are some small buildings that I see people walking into. People walk around holding some of the things Devin and I saw on the TV. They have stuffed animals, candy, and unique-looking foods.

There are stuffed animals so big that some of the kids holding them need their parents' help since they are practically the size of the kids. Some game booths have stuffed animals hanging on the walls or ceilings. Each animal is a different color. No stuffed animal is the standard color they're supposed to be. There are some dogs that are bright purple and snakes that are neon pink.

I have to take a moment to pinch myself to make sure that this is real. When my pinch doesn't wake me up, I know this is reality. I take another look around the place, and then I look at my Dad and Devin, both of their faces are full of amazement, just like mine. When Mom hears about this, she is going to regret not coming.

I try to figure out what we should do first when I finish soaking everything in and getting my thoughts back together. There is so much to do here that I don't know where to start. We only have one night, so we have to make it count. The advertisement made it clear that the carnival would only be here for one day.

As if reading my mind, Devin says, "Why don't we start on the right side and make our way around the place." I agree, and the three of us make our way to the stand with the shark heads.

After a round of people are done and move to their next game, the three of us take the first three seats, and a few other people join us. I am sitting on the end, and when I look over to everyone else sitting down the line, I can see they are just as thrilled to be here as I am. This is our first game tonight, and I am having trouble containing my excitement. I hope it is as fun as it looks.

"Welcome to Shoot the Shark! The rules are simple, aim your water gun at the shark's mouth and shoot. The first person to get the shark's head to the top wins! Please begin by inserting your card in the slot by your seat." The woman standing in the game booth says with a big smile on her face. I notice that she is wearing the same uniform as the man at the entrance.

I look down at my seat and insert my card into the machine. Devin and my Dad do the same.

"Great! Now that everyone has inserted their cards, the game will begin in ten seconds! When you hear the music start, that means the game has begun, so make sure you are ready!"

Both Devin and I look at each other and get our guns ready to aim at the shark's mouth. After ten seconds, a bell is heard, music starts playing, and the lights start to shine different colors really fast around the stand. I shoot the gun at the shark, and the head slowly begins to rise. It is sometimes hard to hit it directly in the mouth, but I focus and try to move my gun up at the same slow speed as the head rising.

Everyone's shark is doing about the same, but when someone misses the mouth, they fall behind everyone else's. Devin and I are almost neck and neck, so I focus on keeping the gun straight and hope he messes up. My heart races with anticipation. I want to win, but I can tell that Devin is doing about the same as me, and I will have to do better to beat him.

To my left, I see my Dad's shark head start to get a lead above ours before it slows, and my shark head passes his. As we get closer to the top, I notice my shark slowly moving past Devins and the others. My shark's head reaches the top first, and a loud bell is rung. The fast music starts to play for a second before stopping. I can still hear the music from the games around us, but it is quiet enough to hear the woman speak.

"Congratulations to this young woman over here! Now, everyone may remove their card from the machine."

I can't help but jump up in excitement, knowing that I won the first game. Although there are still a lot more games to be played, this win will help give me confidence for the next game.

Our cards pop out of the machine, and we grab them. The smiling woman at the stand hands me a small chocolate bar for winning, and I take it with excitement. Candy is hard to get in our town and is typically reserved for special occasions, so I share it with Devin before we move on to the next stand.

At this stand, we find a small pool of water with floating jars on top. The people at the stand look to be throwing little balls at the jar, but only a few are making it into them. When someone makes a ball into the jar, the rim lights up a bright green. When they are done throwing and their turn is done, all the jars return to normal, and the woman collects the balls out of them.

"Looks like you're going to lose this one, Sam," Devin says smugly. He's always been better at games that involve throwing.

"Don't listen to him, Sam. Just focus on where you want the ball to go, and you will do fine." My Dad says, but I know I'm not going to win this one.

We watch a few more people go before it becomes our turn. "Who's first?" the woman at the stand asks.

"Sam."

"Devin."

I glare at Devin, and he just gives me a smile. "You won the last game. That means you should go first."

"You just want to see me fail so you can make fun of me," I state as I walk up and insert my card into the small machine on the side.

"You get ten balls to try and throw into any of the floating jars." The woman says as she hands me a few of the balls. Each one is a different color, and they are pretty small, so I am able to hold three of them in my hand at once. I take a deep breath and throw my first one at the closest jar. It misses.

I can hear Devin chuckle behind me, and I just roll my eyes. I throw the next one, and it does the same. I would like to make one in and shut Devin up, but that doesn't seem very likely at the moment.

"Try aiming at the jar and making it in," Devin says. Such a helpful little brother. I can't believe I never thought of that, I think to myself sarcastically. I want to throw one of the balls at his head, but I would probably accidentally hit an innocent bystander with my bad aim.

I look directly at the closest glass jar and throw another ball, and another, and another. They all miss the jar. I let out a sigh and throw another in frustration. Tink, it hits off of the side of one of the jars.

"Now she's getting somewhere," my Dad says with a small smile.

I am not getting anywhere since I have no idea how I did that. I try doing the same thing as before by using my frustration, and this time, it actually makes it in.

The rim of the jar turns green, and I jump up in excitement, "See, I'm not completely bad at this game!" I say while turning around fast to Devin. He just puts his hands up in surrender while rolling his eyes. I quickly turn around and throw another, and it hits off the side of the jar. I have two balls left.

I throw the one again at the closest jar, and it barely misses. I am down to my last one. I take another deep breath, concentrate, and throw.

CHAPTER 3

The ball makes it in.

"I got two in! While that's not great, it is still better than nothing," I exclaim to my brother. I am thoroughly impressed with myself for doing that. I thought I would ultimately do terribly, but two out of ten is better than zero out of ten.

The woman at the booth presses something on a small tablet I just now noticed, and then my card pops out slightly from the machine. I take my card back and move out of the way for Devin.

"Let me show you how it's done," he inserts his card, and the woman hands over the ten balls. The first ball goes right into one of the jars floating in the middle, but his second throw bounces off the top of the jar. He continues to throw them, and in the end, he makes eight out of the ten jars, and I make a very annoyed face. At least we are now tied with one win for me and one win for Devin.

He turns around with a smug smile, and I do my best to ignore him and watch our Dad. He misses the first two but makes the third. On his fourth shot, he throws the ball right into the jar, but it bounces out. We laugh about it for a moment before he throws the rest of the balls. In the end, he makes three into the jars, but I know he could have done better.

Since that game is just for fun and was individually played, there is no winner. Therefore, there is no prize, and we move on to the next game.

The next game is more of a table stand rather than the usual bigger stands and booths that surround the carnival, and it requires two people to play. This is a game I am very familiar with since Devin, and I used to play it a lot as kids. The game is arm wrestling, and my brother immediately looks over to my Dad to challenge him in the game.

They both insert their cards and when the woman at the stand says go, they both begin their struggle to push the other one's arm down. Both of them are strong, and there is a lot of back-and-forth struggling, so it is hard to tell who is doing better.

I see the determination in Devin's face. His brows come together in concentration, and his face starts to get a little red the longer the competition goes on. Dad, on the other hand, looks like he is not even breaking a sweet. Ultimately, Devin wins, and he gets excited once again. The lady hands him a piece of chocolate, and we move on.

We play two other games before coming to the next one, which takes place in a building that I know was not there before the carnival was put up. I wonder how much time and money they spent making the carnival for us. I also wonder if we will get more things like this. Maybe the Governors will open this carnival once a month or something, or perhaps it doesn't have to be for just one night.

The sign out front of the building says Mirror Maze in sharp letters. We get in line and wait. Devin is still teasing me about the throwing game and how he could have easily beaten me in arm wrestling if I had played, and I tease him about his lack of directional skills. The game has the word maze in the name, and I know that it means a sense of direction will be needed.

"Remember the first time you came home from school without Mom? You were so sure that you didn't have to take a left turn out of the school that you ended up going straight to the Jefferson's house five blocks away," I say, and we all laugh.

"How many times do I have to tell you? I saw my friend Evan, and I started walking without thinking. I made it home eventually."

"Yeah, eventually being the keyword," I say. We all laugh again, and the line moves up a little more.

I think about how Mom made me walk Devin home every day from school for a whole month after that. To make things interesting, Devin and I wouldn't just walk home, that would be too boring. Instead, we would race each other to the big tree at the end of our driveway. I was always the fastest, but I made sure to run slower so that Devin wouldn't lose me and get lost again.

Every few minutes, the line would move up when they let one person in, and eventually, that person would come out of another door to the left of the entrance. Each person seems to spend a different amount of time in there, but they always come out after about four to eight minutes.

When it comes to our turn, we follow the same system as before and let Devin, the reigning champion, go first since he won the last game.

Devin enters his card into the slot by the door and goes in. I immediately turn to face my Dad and address what he's been doing, "You can stop now, you know."

"Stop what?" He says while still looking at the door.

"I know you have been letting us win. I saw you in the shark game. You were winning but pulled away. Then there was the throwing game, where I know you could have done better, but you did badly to make me feel better. I also know you could have kicked Devin's ass in arm wrestling."

"I have no idea what you're talking about," he says innocently, but I know better. He wants us to believe that we are good at things in order to give us the confidence to continue trying more and believe in ourselves.

The only time he doesn't do this is when Devin and I are doing something stupid that could potentially get us hurt. My Mom once said that he just wants us to challenge ourselves so that we will be prepared for anything in the future.

After a few minutes, the woman in uniform opens the door and instructs me to insert my card then come inside. I give one last glance at my Dad to make sure he knows that I know what he's doing, and then I do as the woman told me to. I insert my card into the machine and then walk through the glass door that has been tinted so that no one on the outside can see what is on the inside.

The room is silent with dark walls, but there is an open doorway that is lit up with bright lights around the rim of it. I can see a small amount of the way inside the door, and from what I can tell, there are full-length mirrors inside.

"You are to find your way out of this maze of mirrors. Please try not to touch or break any of the mirrors or decoys." Decoys? "Once you finish, remember to take your card back at the exit. You may now enter."

Her serious voice and disinterested expression lead me to believe that she will not answer any questions I may have about what she means by decoys.

I enter through the illuminated doorway and immediately notice my reflection staring back at me, so I know a mirror is in front of me. I look to my left and right. I can see my reflection standing further away to the left, so that is the direction I go.

While I am walking, I make sure to stay within the walls of my reflection and head toward the direction where I am not seen. This seems simple, so I start walking a little faster. I believe that I am walking in the right direction because I see my reflection farther away, but all of a sudden, I go to take another step, and I am blocked by an invisible wall. The invisible wall is clear glass.

I put my hand to the glass and immediately assume this is what the woman meant by decoy. I then move to the side where my hand touches the mirror and try to find where I am supposed to go. I put my hand out, and when it feels nothing, I continue that way.

I walk into a few more decoy paths and find myself sometimes stuck in corners and having to go back the other way. The whole thing seems really confusing.

I stop for a second to take a closer look at the mirrors and decoy glass and see that there is a difference between the two. On the bottom, there is about an inch of a white outline around both the mirror and glass. On the mirror, I can see the small outline reflection of the light, whereas on the decoys, the outline does not reflect. Looking at this helps me see which way is a dead end and which way will lead me out of here.

I continue to look at the outline of the maze for a while. This method makes me move through the maze quickly, and I don't walk into any more decoys. I am doing pretty well with this tactic until I turn a corner and nearly have a heart attack.

Instead of seeing myself standing in front of me, there is somebody else, and it's not my brother or anyone I know. A boy no older than me is just standing there. He is wearing a gray shirt with a hole in the shoulder and it has a handful of stains and dirt on it.

I immediately know he is not from Treegrass. Not only have I never seen him before in my life, but everyone in our town always wears nice, clean, and washed clothes. Therefore, nobody should look like him.

The boy has a small cut on his cheek and is thin, a lot thinner than he should be. I look away from him and around at my surroundings. There is no one else here. I regain my composure and look at him again.

That is when he says something that makes my blood run cold.

"Run."

CHAPTER 4

I stay standing in the same spot, staring at him like an idiot.

This guy could be here to kill me, and my dumb ass is just standing in place as if I would allow him to. Maybe I should let him kill me. It would only be natural selection doing its job. If I am stupid enough to stand in place while someone who clearly looks like he just ran through the woods for a whole month trying to escape a murderer, or is a murderer tells me to run, then it is only fitting that I should be taken out of this world.

"Run, you have to leave this place!" He yells.

The urgency in his voice snaps me out of whatever trance that was keeping me grounded, and it makes me want to do exactly what he says.

I quickly look around me and remember where I am. The mirrors and decoys would make it hard to get out of here fast. If I try to run, I would just go straight into another decoy glass wall, but maybe that's what he wants. I relax a little bit. This is just a joke, he wants to see me run straight into a wall so he can laugh.

I take another look at the boy, the dark circles under his eyes, his slumped shoulders, and the look in his eyes that says listen to me. He's not joking.

Shit.

"Go! Leave! Get out of here!" He yells on the other side of the glass.

"Get out of the carnival!" His voice sounds muffled, but it still scares me enough to take a step back and make the logical decision to find my way out of here.

It takes me a second to gather my thoughts, and once I do, I realize that doing the same thing I was doing before is probably my best option for leaving this place. I keep my eyes glued to the bottom of the mirrors and decoys until I eventually find myself running through this maze. Left, left, right, left, right, right, right, left, now there is a door in front of me.

I push the door open quickly and run out of the maze. Once I am standing outside again, I am greeted by the bright colors and loud music from the carnival. The cool air of early spring hits me, and that's when I noticed how hard I must have been running.

"Don't forget to take your card," an unfamiliar voice says.

I look to my left and see Devin standing there waiting for me. I look over by the door, and my card pops out of the machine. I slowly take it out and walk over to Devin.

"Did you see that boy in there?" I ask him.

"No," he says, and by the calm look on his face, I know he is telling the truth. "But you look like you have seen a ghost."

"There was a boy in there, no older than me, Devin. He was yelling at me to run. He was scaring me."

He looks at me with concern for a moment, "Maybe he was a decoy. I don't know about you, but the lady giving me the rules didn't want to specify what the decoys were. She kept telling me to go inside and that I would find out once I was in there. I think she was talking about the glass, but maybe she was also talking about the boy too."

That's a good point, but it still isn't a good enough reason to scare the crap out of me. "He told me to get out of the carnival," I tell Devin.

"Maybe he was trying to hit on you, you know. Maybe he was trying to be like, 'Hay, you should get out of the carnival and go out with me instead,'" Devin says in a deeper and odd kind of voice.

I punch his arm and give him a fake laugh, "That was so not what he meant."

"Really, because I have seen plenty of guys ask you out in some of the weirdest ways. It is honestly pretty comical to watch. They can make a show about it."

"Shut up. If he really was a decoy, then why didn't you see him."

"I don't know, maybe he was too busy yelling at someone else or freaking out other easy targets like yourself."

I am about to say how I am not an easy target when the exit door opens and my Dad comes out. He takes his card from the machine and walks over to us.

"Hey, kiddos, where to next?"

Maybe Devin is right, and I am just overreacting to something that's supposed to be fun. Devin looks at me, and I put a slight smile on my face and point to the next game.

About an hour goes by, and we have played the majority of the games here. There was another throwing game, but this one involved darts and balloons. There was one where we had to roll balls up a hill into designated holes with various points to earn. There was even a rock wall that Devin and I had to try climbing up while hitting buttons on the way, but we both only made it two-thirds of the way to the top before falling. I frankly thought we would do better at it since we grew up climbing trees all the time.

At another stand, we had to watch a guy put something down and place a cup over it. He moved the cups around, and then we had to guess which cup had the object in it. That was easy since it was similar to a game that Devin and I had played together in the past.

Another game involved cups as well, but it was something we ourselves had to do. We had to see who could flip the most cups over in an untraditional way. I won that one since I found a suitable method and stuck to it.

Our favorite was the one where we got to smack a stuffed rat's head when it popped out one of the nine holes on a board. We liked it so much that we played it twice, and each time, Devin and I did so well that the man running the booth was very impressed and said that we were only a few points away from one another.

We take a break from playing the games and walk over to a line of tents set up, each one serving a different kind of food.

The first tent we go up to has a grill going. They are making hotdogs and hamburgers, but they have a lot more options for top-pings than I am used to seeing. Devin and I both get hamburgers with cheese, bacon, and tomato, which is not typical in our town but it tastes terrific. It makes me wonder if this is common in other towns or if the carnival will be the first time they experience these things too.

Our Dad asks for a hotdog, and the guy taking our order asks if he would like any relish on it. The three of us look at him as if he has five heads. The guy explains that it's something you can put on the hotdog and gives my Dad a sample of it. After trying it, my Dad says yes to putting that on his hotdog, and then he turns to the two of us to tell us that the relish has a different taste than anything he has ever eaten before.

The next tent had six different ice cream flavors. We didn't try them since we didn't want to get too full. Besides, we already have an ice cream shop in our town that we can visit anytime. It may not have the same flavors, but it's still good.

While walking around, we keep hearing people talk about a Ferris wheel and how fun it is to go on. We grab some hot chocolate that is so good I want to buy a whole gallon of it. They must use a different ingredient than we do, and I wish I knew what it was. Then we make our way to the Ferris wheel.

The Ferris wheel is massive. We saw it while walking around but did not know what it was called or what it did. It is exceptionally tall and lit with lights that simultaneously change color every few seconds. We see people getting out of and into large buckets that look to be hand-painted.

We quickly get in line and stare at the giant circle that is slowly rotating above us. The ride stops every few minutes to let people out and to let new people in. Once the new people are on, the ride makes two full circles before stopping to repeat the cycle of letting people out and on.

It gets to our turn, and the three of us all get into one of the buckets

"When you get to the top, make sure to look that way." A guy in uniform points to my right. "You're going to see a big tent. They are having a big surprise there at nine o'clock and don't want anyone to miss it." The guy then closes the bucket door, and we thank him.

After they get everyone else into their own buckets, we start moving. As we go up, I can see the sun just finish setting on the horizon, all the colors in the sky look so beautiful. I wish it could stay like this forever.

Chapter 5

When we reach the top, I can see the whole carnival and more. All the lights make the view look spectacular, and it almost feels as if I am in a dream. It's darker around the outside of the carnival, but I am still able to make out the outline of trees in the distance and the town border.

The town border is just a fortified chain fence for the most part, it holds all twelve thousand of us Treegrass people in place to protect us from any potential threats. After the war, the government made sure to enclose each town so that if anyone like our old enemy, the Fritts, came they couldn't take our homes. The Fritts were defeated in the war, but that does not mean there aren't more people out there who want what we have.

The parts of our town that are located by the tree line, like we are now, are protected by a chain fence since not many people like going into the woods to try and break in. Other parts of our town are protected with high walls that are covered in colorful murals on the inside. The murals make the walls look less scary, and the school art teachers always like taking trips to the wall to show us the beautiful work the artists have done in the past.

"Look, that must be the big tent that guy was talking about."

Devin and I look over to where my Dad is pointing, and sure enough, there is a big tent. The tent has lights going vertically up the tent from the ground. They change color in unison, making the tent stand out, and it definitely makes me want to know what is inside.

"Any guesses as to what the surprise will be?" My Dad asks, knowing how much we like this game.

I think about it for a moment before guessing, "I think it's going to be some kind of special show. The 155th anniversary of the end of the New World-Fritt War is coming up in two months, maybe it could be a show dedicated to that history."

The New World has been around for 172 years, and we will be celebrating 173 years in the winter. The war between the New World and the Fritts started only two years after we officially became a country, and it lasted for almost sixteen years. Many people at the time thought it would last even longer than that since neither side was making much progress.

Devin thinks about it some more and then makes his guess, "Well, I think it has something to do with the cards. I don't know if you noticed, but they only matter in the games, not the food or this ride. I think they're going to have a small show, and then they're going to announce the top three players and maybe give them their own special rewards."

We all look at each other. Both guesses would be pretty cool, but the only way we will know who is right or closer to the right answer is if we go.

"So we can go at nine?" I ask my Dad.

He looks at me, "I promised not to get you two home too late."

Devin and I look at each other and then back at our Dad with our best puppy dog eyes. I may not be a little kid anymore, but the puppy dog eyes never stop working.

"Fine. If it starts at nine and is only about an hour, then that shouldn't be too late to get home. And besides, it's Friday. It's not like you have school tomorrow, so your Mom can't get mad at me," Dad says while looking at Devin.

I have work tomorrow morning, but I don't point that out. I am an adult now, I can make decisions for myself, and I decide that I want to stay here until we get kicked out at the end of the night.

Devin and I look at each other triumphantly and try to give our Dad a big hug. The bucket we are in tilts, and we sit back down in our seats, not wanting to break the ride and fall to our deaths. I know he would have let us go find out what is in the tent even if we did not use our charms on him, he's good like that.

The ride makes another complete rotation before coming to a stop at the bottom, where we get off. I can't believe how amazing this night has gone so far, and it's not even over.

We continue our method of going in order of the games, and the next one up isn't really a game but a question.

There is a drawing of a triangle made up of other triangles in front of us. The lady says to insert our cards and type our guesses on the tablet on the table when we are ready. She said that we are guessing how many triangles we think are in the image.

I begin trying to count how many there are, but it's tricky since you can't write on it to outline the ones you can see, and some of the triangles make other triangles.

I step up to the table, insert my card into the tablet, and place my guess. Devin looks at me and then back at the problem with concentration. After another minute, he goes to the table and places his guess, and so does my Dad.

"What number did you guess Sam?" Devin asks.

"Twenty-four, you?"

Devin looks at me, contemplating, then answers, "Twenty-two. How did you get twenty-four?"

I point to the triangle, trying my best to explain my thought process. "There are the obvious big triangles and smaller ones, but then the smaller ones make up medium sized ones, and I just kept looking at them in a bunch of different ways."

Devin looks at me in understanding, and then we both turn to our Dad

"What did you guess, old man?" Devin says.

"Twenty-five, one more than Sam here."

The woman is not allowed to tell us the answer, so we move on. As we are walking, I catch the sight of a short gray haired lady walking by. I figure it is not polite to ignore her, so I decide to give her a smile and say, "Hi Ms. Betty, how are you?"

She turns around and smiles. "Samantha! I'm doing fine. I decided to come see my grandkids and have fun for a bit, but it's getting late now so I think I am going to head home now. It's good to see you. Is this your brother Devin? He's gotten so tall." We talk for a few minutes, but I know if I don't make up an excuse to leave, then we will be here all night.

I tell her that my father and brother are waiting on me which is not a complete lie. They are standing a few feet away from us, discussing the triangle debate again.

"Well, that's all right. Have a good night, and I'll see you next week, Ms. Betty."

"Goodnight Samantha," she says back with a wave.

A security guard seems to hear this and comes up to us.

"Are you sure you are leaving so soon? The surprise is going to start shortly," the guard asks, sounding disappointed but holding a friendly smile.

"I wish I could stay, but I would probably fall asleep and miss the whole thing, but thank you anyway," Ms. Betty says, and both the security guard and I understand.

"Well, then, in that case, how about I walk you out?" the guard offers, and Ms. Betty accepts. We say goodbye again, and I watch as the two walk towards the exit.

"Come on Sam, we have time for one more game before the show," Devin says in a rush.

We move to the last game, where the woman instructs that you and an opponent hold on to a bar for as long as you can without touching the ground or letting go. The first one to let go loses, and the winner gets to pick a stuffed animal. My Dad sits this one out while Devin and I go up against each other.

We insert our cards and grab the bar. Since I'm barely five feet three inches, I have to use a little stepping stool to grab the bar. I know Devin is going to win since he is a lot stronger than me, but I have to try anyway.

I hold onto the bar, and someone takes the stool away as the woman starts the clock. I am facing Devin and he looks comfortable hanging onto the bar with his feet slightly lifted up so he doesn't touch the ground on accident. At first, it's not so bad until the woman states that we have been holding on for about thirty-five seconds. That's when I start to feel it.

My arms begin to feel uncomfortable, and they get a burning sensation. I try to hold on for a few more seconds, but my hands get sweaty, and I lose my grip and drop.

"Great job guys! The winner goes to this young gentleman over here."

I look at the clock, and it is stopped at forty-seven seconds. I think the clock is wrong because it felt a lot longer than that.

Devin gets to pick a stuffed animal, and he chooses the green bunny. "I'll give it to Mud," he says, and I kind of guessed he would do that since neither of us has played with stuffed animals since we were kids.

We have just been giving away all of the other toys we won tonight to other little kids we see walking around, but there are none in the area right now. Everyone must be at the big show tent for the surprise.

My Dad claps his hands together and looks at us, "So, is it time to go to the surprise?"

We both nod in agreement and walk towards the big, illuminated tent.

"I wonder whose guess is going to win," I say.

Chapter 6

The three of us walk towards the brightly lit tent along with hundreds of other people from our town. Each person who walks into the tent has a big smile on their face, especially the kids. Everyone is having as good a night, just like the three of us, and I pinch myself once again just to make sure that I am not going to wake up and learn that this was just a dream.

The carnival is a kaleidoscope of games, candy, colorful lights, and food. It is an overload of excitement that makes me wish that every day could be like this. Maybe not every day, but I would be happy if the carnival was a monthly affair. Treegrass is great, but it gets boring sometimes. If the government were to allow more events like this, then I would be ecstatic.

At the entrance, about ten security guards are taking people's cards and putting them in small black boxes. When we get closer, we hear the guy explaining that our cards will be put into the box, and we will hold onto them until further instruction. He says the reason for this will be explained at the end of the surprise. We do as instructed and walk in.

The inside of the tent is bright, with big lights pointing down from the ceiling. There are long rows of benches that go up what looks to be fifteen layers. The benches encircle the center of the room, but there are four open spaces between the groups of benches for the doors. The first two doors are the doors we came through to get into here, and I assume that the other two led to the back of the tent for the workers.

Below each bench, there is a strip of white light, which makes the wooden benches look much brighter. Most people are already sitting down, but we find a spot on the third layer of benches closer to the door we came through.

We can easily see over the heads of the little kids sitting in front of us. They look to be between the ages of five and ten. Their parents sit on the end, holding a handful of stuffed animals. Their boxes containing their cards sit next to them on the bench, just like my Dad's and Devin's. I chose to hold mine just in case Devin tries to mess with it or take it.

Devin lifts his box up off the bench and holds it up in front of me with a mischievous glint in his eyes. "It looks like this surprise has something to do with the cards, like I guessed," he says.

Of course, Devin's guess seems to be the right one, so he stands a good chance at winning this guessing game, but I don't necessarily think I'm wrong either.

I shoot Devin a glare, "Maybe, but the night is still young. Anything can happen."

Anything can happen. It has been a fantastic night so far, and I don't think it will end anytime soon. We have experienced so many new things today, and I think this surprise could be another.

We sit for a few minutes in our seats, and I take the opportunity to take in the whole place. It's so bright. The colorful lights somehow look more vibrant in here than they did outside. The inside tent walls are white, but there are long lights that make the tent appear to be any color they want.

There is an open space in the middle of the room with solid white flooring, it shines so brightly that I can see the reflection of some people walking by in it. Just like the white tent, the white floor looks as though it is changing color because of the lights as well.

I don't get much longer to look around because the lights dim until the only light is in the center of the room. Everyone gets quiet. The children in front of us happily mutter something to one another, and their parents quickly shush them.

Similar reactions happen all around us. Even adults can't take their eyes off the center of the room. We all wait impatiently for it to begin. I stare at the center, looking for a sign of anything happening.

Then it starts.

At first, it's just a few specks of light floating individually, but eventually, they all come together to form the shape of an elephant. I remember learning in school that elephants are an endangered species, with only a few remaining in the world.

The elephant is lit up blue, and the tiny lights move to make it appear as though the elephant is walking across the room. A small baby elephant emerges from underneath the first elephant, and soon enough, there are multiple holographic elephants in the tent.

The elephants throw up their trunks, and a loud sound is heard throughout the tent. They walk slowly in a circle, and as they get closer to us, I can see so much more detail in them. Their whole body is covered in the tiny lights. There are even smaller lights that are put together to make the elephant's eyes, and I find myself wondering how on earth they were able to do this.

The elephants eventually leave by their light fading out but other animals quickly replace them, each one a different color.

The holograms of these animals in bright lights are amazing. Soft music plays over the sounds of each animal, making the experience feel more alive and magnificent. At some point there are various birds flying around the whole tent and over people's heads.

Red horses come running into the circle out of nowhere. The horses run in a circle for a few minutes, their hair blowing perfectly until they, too, disappear and are replaced by tigers.

The tigers look scary in the most beautiful way. I think they might be my favorite so far.

They are projected with different colored lights to make up the pattern on their fur. Each strand of hair must be made out of at least four different floating lights because it looks real and fluffy. I wish I could walk up to them and run my fingers through their fur. A woman walks out, and one of the tigers circles her. She holds a hoop in one hand and lifts it up. One of the tigers sees this and runs at the hoop, jumping perfectly through it.

Everyone, including me, is amazed by this and starts clapping. The woman does this repeatedly from different heights, and I can't take my eyes away.

The woman is then handed a different hoop and walks to the other side of the tent. She stops for a minute, and right before she puts the hoop above her head, she lights it on fire. The tiger doesn't seem to be phased, maybe because it's just a hologram, but it runs and jumps through the hoop regardless.

I know that the tigers are not real and that there was no real danger from the fire, but I am amazed. I feel like they are real, and I am watching all of these animals in their natural habitat, not just in some tent. I wish they would play this on the TV every night so I could watch it over and over again.

People start clapping even more, and I find myself doing the same.

The tigers and the women exit the circle, and for a minute, the room is covered in darkness before a new hologram appears in the center. This time, it does not include any animals. It is a hologram of the war.

"It has been almost 155 years since the end of the great war between the New World and Fritt Land," a loud male's voice says. The lights move to form a moving image of men firing guns at one another.

I elbow Devin, "Told you it has something to do with the anniversary of the New World and the Fritts." Devin gives me a quick glance over to me before focusing back on the show.

The specks of light move apart and then back together to form a new image of the three heads of government at the time. Together they talk urgently about how the Fritts are trying to take our land and resources for themselves.

We learned in school that many years before the war started, there were a lot of countries that did not use their resources appropriately, and it had devastating effects. There were shortages of food and housing that caused many people to riot and set fires to government buildings and innocent people's homes.

Our government was run by a single leader at the time, but after the rioting, there was a revolution that led to us having three heads of government and forming an all new country called the New World.

The three heads of government are now represented today as Governor Alfred Wood, Governor Arthur Davies, and Governor Audrey Lewis. Each of them work together to make decisions and come up with solutions for the New World, while this has worked in bringing our country out of starvation and destruction, other countries were not so lucky.

Places like Fritt Land resorted to taking other people's resources rather than fixing themselves so they could produce goods on their own. I think that is part of the reason people have hated the Fritts.

They didn't just hate them because they made us go to war and risk the lives of our people, but because they could have done exactly what we did and changed. They could have listened to their people, identified the problems, and come up with solutions. I guess one good thing that came out of the war was that the New World saw what damage other people could do and built proper walls and protection from crazy people like the Fritts.

The New World didn't solve its problems overnight. They listened to the people and came up with ways to ration our resources long enough to find a better long term solution.

We didn't choose to go to war.

Chapter 7

The lights change again to show the three heads of government at the time. This time, they are addressing the country about going to war with the Fritts to keep what we worked so hard for.

The lights then move to show the fighting in different areas of our country, one being in Treegrass. Men hid behind the rubble of old buildings, only popping their heads out occasionally to fire their weapons.

One man shoots a Fritt, and the Fritt bursts into tiny white lights until he is no longer there. Some men have tiny lights pouring out of them as they walk by. It looks pretty, but I know this is just the government's way of protecting us from seeing the actual blood and horror of the war.

The following image shows men and women cheering in the streets, "Today is a day of celebration. The New World has finally defeated its greatest enemy, the Fritts. We have fought every last one of them so that they shall never return to harm us anymore. Today, we are free of fear, we are free of starvation, and we are free to become the best we can hope to be," says the familiar voice of Governor Joseph Johnson, one of the country's favorite Governors at the time of the war.

Cheers and claps are heard in the tent once again before it quiets back down. The room goes dark for a few moments, and we are left waiting in anticipation. Then lights form to show the head of one of our current day governors, Governor Davies, in the center of the room.

"Dear people of Treegrass, I hope you had fun today here at the carnival. Setting up such an event was not easy, but we hope it was all worth it. My fellow Governors and I wanted to give you all a special night before delivering some unpleasant news."

My heart sinks a little at the sound of that. What does he mean by unpleasant news? Has something happened in one of the other towns? Is there a new threat?

He takes a moment before speaking again, "As many of you know, the New World has been through a lot. We have seen famine, revolutions, wars and overall a lot of destruction. We have been able to overcome all of this and make the New World safe for everyone, or so we thought," Governor Davies takes a deep breath and looks down for a moment before looking at us again.

"It is with deep sadness that I must inform you of our country's struggles in recent years. For over a century, we have been able to avoid falling back into a shortage of food and resources, but we were informed two years ago that that would not be the case for long. Over those two years, your government has worked hard to find possible ways to avoid such a disaster, and we think we have found one."

"It has come to our attention that it is not that we are short on our average yearly number of produce, but it is the number of people in the towns that are growing. This population growth has made us use valuable land for homes instead of crops. The building of homes has caused a shortage of valuable resources. The threat of outsiders has prevented us from expanding town borders, so your fellow Governors and I have had to think long and hard about our options."

"Every day, we have asked ourselves, how do we fix this? One option is to risk our lives and expand our town borders to gain more land to grow food and housing. Unfortunately, even if this option were not dangerous, it would take years, and by then, hundreds or thousands of people could die a slow starving death."

Governor Davis says this last part slowly as if to ensure that everyone understands that they do not wish for this to happen and that starving would be a terrible way to die.

"With much debate, we came up with another option. We go from town to town and give everyone a night to remember before reducing the population peacefully. Each person who walked into the carnival was handed a card with their name on it, and now you hold a box containing your card and the score of how well you did here tonight."

People around us start looking at one another before quiet chatter starts up. What could scorecards have to do with helping the New World's problems, and what did he mean by reducing the population peacefully?

"We have averaged those scores to tell us the top fifty percent of the people in Treegrass. Some of the games you played here tonight tested your strength, while most tested your intelligence.

Your scores were also weighted. If you are seventeen or younger, you get a twenty-point bonus. If you are older than fifty, then you get a twenty-point reduction. Anyone who did not play any games got zero points."

"The people who are in the top fifty percent are safe and will live out the rest of their lives safely in Treegrass. To the people who do not make the top fifty, you will be given a moment with your family and loved ones. Then you will be instructed to follow the security guards to a separate room where you will not experience a slow death like the many who died in the famine."

What? This can't be real. It has to be some sort of twisted joke. One of our Governors did not just insinuate that they are going to kill half of our town. That can't be right. Someone's going to come out here any second and tell us that this is just a misunderstanding. This can't be real.

Other people must start coming to the same conclusion as me because the chatter becomes louder, and people start looking panicked.

"Everyone's score has been accounted for when you put your cards in the box, so we know who the top fifty percent of your town is. Those of you who are in the top fifty percent will see a green light in the corner of your box, while the ones who fell below the fifty percent mark will see a red light."

I look down at my box, and sure enough, there is a small green light in the corner. I look at Devin's and it's the same. Then it hits me. Dad, he purposely lost the games. I look over at his box.

Red.

No. He lost the games on purpose. No, that's not fair. It's not fair. They can't do that.

This is just a misunderstanding. They aren't actually going to kill half the town. They can't do that, right? They must have morals, too. There is no way the three heads of government felt that the solution to this problem would be murdering their own people.

My heart starts racing as I begin to think about it more. You will not experience a slow death like the many who died in the famine. Does that mean they plan on killing half the town quickly? Are they moving them somewhere else? What do they mean?

The Governor's head disappears, and the lights are turned back on. A loud, demanding voice is heard, "If you have a box containing a red light in the corner, please come to the center of the room now."

The people around us start to get up from their seats, but only a few move to the center of the room.

"Where are you bringing them?"

"Are you really going to kill off half the town?"

"Answer my question! Look at me! You can't do this!"

My Dad grabs my hand and then reaches over to Devin to grab him as well. "We are leaving. Now," he says. It is not a question, and my brother and I don't fight him on the matter.

We walk down the now crowded stairs and try making our way to the exit. People start pushing and shoving to get to the front, so I hold onto my Dad's hand tighter so we do not get separated. As we make little progress towards the front, we hear people shouting to open the doors.

"Let us out!"

"You can't keep us in here. We have families!"

"Open the door, or you will regret it!" A loud angry man yells.

More people start shouting, "Let us out! Let us out!"

They locked us in.

People rush to the center of the room, where a number of armed guards are now standing, and try to demand they tell us what they are planning to do with the people with red lights on their boxes. The guards do not answer. All they do is stand there and ask for the people with red lights on their boxes to come to the center.

One man gets right up in a guard's face and demands that he answer the questions, and when the guard does not, the man pushes the guard. The guard stumbles back but does not fall. Others join in and start getting up in other guards' faces and pushing and shoving them when they get no answer.

When this continues, the guards ask for everyone to calm down, but no one is listening anymore. Then, right when one guy is about to punch a guard, a gunshot is heard, and the guy falls to the ground, fist still in the air. It is dead silent for a second as everyone watches as the guy's shirt becomes covered in blood.

That is when the real chaos erupts.

Chapter 8

People start screaming and yelling in a panic. I look around us, but no one seems to know what to do.

Some people are running in circles, bumping into one another, while others are still sitting down in their seats in shock. A number of people have dropped their boxes on the ground, but I know the security guards can just look at the names on the boxes and find out who they are. Devin's stuffed bunny for Mud is long gone in the crowd of scared people and has probably been trampled over.

I look around to see if there could somehow be another exit we could use to get out of here, but there isn't.

We remain standing on the bottom of the benches. I look at my Dad, and I can see him looking around the place for a way out, just like I was. I can see the fear in his face, but he is not panicking, which helps me not panic.

A tall guy comes running past us towards the locked exit, pushing me down in the process. My Dad reaches a hand out for me to take, and I hold onto it once more.

"Are you alright, Sam?" He asks.

"Yeah," I say, sounding out of breath. I am not sure when or why it got so hard for me to breathe. It gets worse the more I look around at the situation we are in.

People are running anywhere and everywhere in a panic, and the sound of verbal threats and yelling consumes my ears. Another gunshot is heard, then another. I don't see where it was fired from or where it was aiming. I can't seem to focus on anything. There are just too many people moving around in a panic.

I take another look at the room for any possible exit. As I am looking, I am once again pushed by an unfamiliar person, but this time I do not fall. I look over and see that my Dad and Devin are both having the same struggle as me. People keep bumping into them or shoving them to get through to the locked door.

Dad pulls our hands and leads us back onto the bleachers, where we climb up to the sixth row. My eyes start wandering to the bleachers across the way. The white light around the bottom of the seats is still lit, but I catch the sight of red on some of the lower seats. I assume that whoever was sitting or standing there was the target of one of the gunshots that were heard.

More people move down from the top of the bleachers and pass us by. Some are screaming. Others don't say anything out loud, but I know what they are thinking based on their terrified faces.

I see a boy about Devin's age sitting down about three rows up from us. In his hands, he holds a box with a green light. He sees me looking at him, and I can see the panic in his eyes as he quickly hides his box behind his back.

I look back at the center of the room and see that the guards have some people sitting down with their hands behind their backs. I look past them, and my eye catches something in the far back of the room. I can only see a little bit of what is happening, but it looks like a group of people have found a way to get out.

I tug on my Dad's hand, "Look! Dad, look over there! In the back!"

He sees what I'm pointing at, and the three of us start making our way to the back. A group of men are standing behind the bleachers, and they have lifted the tent's tarp to reveal a chain link fence underneath. Each of them starts running over and over again at the same time at the fence.

The fence starts to lean over slightly, and it now has many dents in it. Each of the men do not give up, and Dad tells us to stay put while he joins them. My Dad isn't the biggest person here, but I know he is strong and will do his best to knock the fence over anyway. The more people that join, the faster the fence falls.

With a loud metallic sound, the fence is on the ground, and Dad is grabbing our hands again and leading us over the fallen fence.

Bang

Another bullet is heard being fired. I don't know where it came from or who it was intended for, but I look and see that the three of us are okay before quickly rushing out of the tent with their hands still in mine.

More shots are heard, but we ignore them and run as fast as we can towards nowhere in particular. I see more people running beside us, but no one seems to know where to go.

We just keep running. The only things heard are the sounds of our feet hitting the ground, along with some gunshots. I catch sight of a group of people running together before splitting up and running in different directions, but I don't focus too much on them. I instead focus on where we are going to go. My Dad suddenly yells left, and we all quickly run to the left, where there is a pathway between a few game stands.

When the path reaches the end, Dad pulls us to the right, and we continue running down another pathway. None of this looks familiar now that it's darker out, and I don't have the time to figure out where the exit is.

"Stop now or risk being shot!"

I take a quick glance behind us and see a few guards running after us.

"We have to hide," Devin says. But where? The game stands are small and fully lit up. They would find us there in no time.

We continue running but quickly encounter a problem. While we knocked down the fence that held us in the tent, a large fence still surrounds the whole carnival, and we have just cornered ourselves against it.

Two guards come running towards us, blocking us so we can't move. Dad turns to Devin and me, "Listen to me. You need to run. Find a way out of here, and then warn the rest of the town. Okay? Please do that for me. I love the two of you very much. Okay? Remember that."

He doesn't give us a chance to say anything back. He turns around and runs at the two guards, tackling both of them down to the ground while he screams at us to run.

I quickly grab Devin's hand and run reluctantly past my Dad and the guards on the ground. It is like I can't hear anything anymore. White noise fills my ears, and I can't focus on where we are running anymore. Most likely, we are running away from our Dad, who is probably going to be shot by one of those guards.

We get maybe a few hundred feet before my body feels like it's going to collapse any second. As if sensing this Devin holds me up.

"Sam, look at me. We need to go! Please! Dad's going to be alright, okay? He's smart. He'll get out of this. I just need you to move your feet." I can hear the panic in his voice, and the look on his face matches it.

This seems to be enough to snap me back into reality because I start breathing a little better and start running alongside Devin again without his help. When we reach a darker space in between two games, we take a moment to crouch down so no one can see us.

I notice now that the loud, playful music that once filled the air is gone. I hear the sound of feet hitting the pavement to my right, but I don't dare look in case it's another guard. I poke my head out from around the corner when it quiets down again. The area is clear of people for now, but we can't stay here.

"How the hell do we get out of here, Sam?"

I look at my younger brother. I can tell he's scared but is trying to hold himself together until we get out of here.

"I don't know," is all I can tell him.

I look out of our hiding spot again to try and find a place we could maybe climb onto and then jump the fence, but I have no luck.

I duck back down into our hiding spot and sit there. Devin and I do not say anything to each other. We just sit on the ground and try to catch our breath. Every few minutes, the sound of footsteps is heard, and Devin and I look at each other with panicked eyes.

I wait for about five minutes after the last sound of footsteps is heard, then peek my head out of our hiding spot again. Nothing has changed since the first time I looked, but I keep looking anyway. I am about to turn back to Devin, but my eye catches movement in the distance, and I can't look away.

Across the way, a small group of about fifteen people are sneaking around different stands before they reach a dark path between two food stands. I watch how the person in the back looks around for any guards. I also notice that he looks very familiar.

He's the guy from the Mirror Maze. He catches up with the rest of the group and points across the way to another stand and a building. He stays in the back of the group, and by looking around cautiously at their surroundings, I can tell he is keeping a lookout.

As he skims over the open area before us, and then he catches me watching him.

CHAPTER 9

We stare at each other for a moment, and I see the look of recognition across his face. He remembers me. He looks to the left and then the right before waving me over to him.

I put up a finger to tell him to wait a moment, and then I turn to Devin. "You know that guy I was telling you about earlier, the one yelling at me in the Mirror Maze?"

He looks at me while he thinks for a second, then replies skeptically, "Yeah?"

"He's waving us over across the way. I think we should go," I tell him.

"You think we can trust him? You said he scared you. How do we know he's not planning on killing us?"

"Well, he did tell me to run. Maybe he knows something we don't. It looks like he has a group of people with him, Treegrass people, and I think we should go. We can't stay here."

Devin looks at me for a minute before agreeing.

I look back over to where the mirror guy is and see him waiting. When I start to stand, he quickly puts a hand out to stop us, and we duck down again. A few seconds later, a group of guards walk by. When they pass, we are once again waved over, and I let out a breath that I didn't know I was holding.

I make sure to look for myself to make sure the area is clear before we move quickly over to the other side. Moving out of the darkness into the light makes me feel like anyone can see us, and we will be shot regardless of our score. I realize now that I don't even have my box with me anymore.

When we reach the other side, the mirror guy quickly hides us in the darkness.

"Thought I told you to run earlier." He whispers.

I glare at him, although it's useless in the dark. "How the hell was I supposed to know what you were talking about?" I whisper shout at him, "A random stranger yelling at me to run is not the most reliable reason to do so."

He looks at me for a second with a scowl on his face before motioning us to follow him.

I can't help but ask, "Where are the other people I saw you with before?" I notice they are not here now and I start questioning my decision to come over here.

"They are inside," he replies and walks across the way. I check to make sure no one is coming before I follow him. When Devin and I catch up to the Mirror Maze guy, I notice that we are in a slightly more secluded place.

There is a game booth on one side and a building on the other, making this area like a pathway. There is also a wall dividing us from the rest of the carnival in the back. He stops in front of a door on the side of the building and opens the door. I move to take a step forward to walk in, but my brother stops me.

Devin looks directly at the guy, "How do we know we can trust you?"

The guy looks at Devin for a second before looking around at the place we are in, "How do you really know you can trust anyone? I guess the only thing I can think of to tell you is that the people out here looking for you and I have guns, and we don't."

This seems to be a decent answer for Devin because he nods at me to go in.

Somehow, the room seems darker than the pathway, and I am not able to make out much. It is almost completely pitch black, but as my eyes slowly adjust, I am able to make out some counters and what appears to be people sitting on the ground. I have no idea how big this room is since I can't see far, but I hope it has something we could use to get out of here.

I notice the faint smell of food and realize that he might have brought us to one of the kitchens behind a food stand or something. It's too dark to tell if that is actually where we are, but if it is, then it should be a good place for all of us to hide until we figure everything out.

We join the group and sit down on the ground. After a few moments of silence, someone asks, "What do we do now?" I can't help but agree. What are we doing sitting around here? I doubt the government is going to come to rescue us since they put us in this position.

"We're waiting," says the mirror guy.

Well, that explains nothing. I look at the mirror guy and stare at his outline, contemplating smacking him for the lame answer. He is lucky a voice in the dark speaks instead.

"What are we waiting for exactly?" The voice sounds like it is from an angry woman, and I completely understand why. This has been one stressful night, and waiting around does not seem like the thing to be doing right now.

There are two knocks on the door, and the mirror guy stands up and says, "Him."

He opens the door, and a guy's outline walks through before the door is closed. The two of them come back to the group but don't sit down.

"Find anyone else?" Mirror guy asks the new guy.

"Yeah, I dropped them off outside the maze with Vesper before coming here," the new guy answers.

There is a few seconds of silence after he says this, so I take the opportunity to speak up. "Great, now that the two of you are caught up, would either of you like to catch us up on what the hell is going on," I say, and the two of them look at me questioningly.

"Did you not fill them in on anything?" The new guy asks the mirror guy, and I am starting to get a headache from both of them.

"Well, I told this girl to run earlier, but clearly, she's not a good listener," the mirror guy says, and I am once again ready to smack him.

"Theon, I told you this before. You can't just tell people to run and expect them to listen. You have to explain to them what's going on," the new guy says, sounding annoyed as if they have had this conversation many times before.

Mirror guy, or Theon, as the new guy called him, just shrugs and the new guy decides then to sit down with us and tell us what is going on.

"About two months ago, the government set up a carnival just like this one in our town, Tundris. They promised a night of fun, but at the end of it, they ended up killing sixty percent of the population and then some. Some of us got out and ran south. We found a safe place in the woods a few miles from here."

"We still kept an eye on Tundris, but when we saw the big trucks moving the carnival somewhere else, we decided to send a group to follow it. The trucks stopped at a town a few miles north from here, Redseed. We weren't able to find a way in, but from what we could hear, just like us, the town of Redseed had a great night before the government killed a big number of them, too."

"We found some ATVs we could ride at an abandoned place and took them. When we saw the trucks on the move again, we rode the ATVs behind them, making sure to keep a distance. But we messed up and got lost since we accidentally ended up too far behind them."

"By the time we found out where they were, your town, the carnival had already started." He continues, "We found that there was a way to sneak in through the Mirror Maze. We thought we could walk around the carnival and warn you guys to leave, and that would be it. We learned about an hour before the show that the people who left were just held in a room until everyone's scores were accounted for at the show, then they would be killed depending on those scores."

"We were then trying to find a way to stop the show by cutting the lights, but as you can see, that didn't exactly work. Luckily, you guys are smart and strong and broke the fence. A lot of you got out, but some were taken back to be executed." He sounds defeated when he says this, almost like he blames himself for the governments wrong doing.

"Me, Theon, and a few other people from our old town decided to split up and get as many of you guys out through the maze as we could. This is a pretty big group here, so we're probably going to have to split into two groups to avoid being caught." When he finishes talking, he looks to us for any questions.

The same woman as before speaks up, "Who the hell are you guys?"

"Just some people who are trying to help. We call ourselves the Jumpers, but I guess if you want our actual names, then this here is Theon," he puts a hand on Theon's shoulder and then to himself, "and I'm Aiden, but I don't think right now is the best time to exchange names, we should try getting out of here first."

I think about what he says, is our government really trying to secretly kill us? Have they really been to other towns to reduce the population by killing hundreds, maybe thousands of innocent people? Yes, they are.

I've seen it, haven't I? The way people started to panic in the tent and the way the guards started to shoot people. I've seen the blood they spilled. I believe that what Aiden is saying is true.

No one else seems to have any more questions, so I take that as an unanimous agreement, "Okay, so what's the plan?"

Aiden nods in approval, "Theon here is going to take half of you to the maze first, and I will take the second half of you there a few minutes later. There are many shooters out there looking for anyone, so it's important to stay in the shadows and stay quiet."

I feel like it is obvious but I can't help but ask anyway, "Who are the shooters?"

It is Theon who speaks this time, "The guards with the guns, basically any government official." Well, that's comforting to know, "We should be fine as long as we do what Aiden said and stay in the dark."

"So, who wants to go in the first group?" Aiden asks.

A few people immediately raise their hands and move to the front by Theon. I guess these people are the most desperate to get out of here fast and find their families. I want to see my parents again, too, but I'm willing to let them go first since there will probably only be a small time difference.

After a few more minutes of shuffling around, it is decided that about six people will go with Theon in the first group, and Devin and I will be with the other three in the second group led by Aiden.

Before Theon's group leaves, Aiden reminds him to make sure the coast is clear before leaving.

Theon opens the door, takes a second to assess the situation outside, and then walks out. His group follows him, and we are left in the dark room in silence as we wait for our turn to go.

Chapter 10

It feels like an eternity goes by as we sit in the dark, waiting for Aiden to decide when we should go. No one says anything. The room is so silent that it feels like I can hear my own heart beating as if it were outside of my chest and right next to my ear. I look around the room to see if I can spot anything that could help us as a way to pass the time, but it's useless since it is too dark.

The sudden sound of a gunshot is heard in the distance. The loud noise of the shot makes me jump a little, and I think Devin does the same. At first, it's just a single shot, but then after about thirty seconds, there is the sound of another, and another, and then it's silent again.

After a minute, someone speaks up, "Do you think they're shooting at them?" The voice sounds like it comes from a girl who is young, too young to be in a situation like this. I can't make out the features on her face, but she does not sound familiar.

Most people in our town are strangers to me. There are many familiar faces that I know from walking and biking around town, but I don't actually know who they are. I have only ever made small talk with the people I encounter. When I do make a friend, I hang out with them for a few weeks until our conversations fade to nothing, and they become acquaintances again.

The people here just don't interest me that much. The people I went to school with would rather sit at home and read and reread the same books. They also like redoing the same tasks and rewatching the same shows. I think they believe that if they do something enough times, they will find something new in it, but I think they are just delusional and dull.

That's probably why Devin became my best friend. Not a lot of people in our town like challenging themselves by playing games and trying new things. They are content with doing the same thing over and over again. I guess they have to be right. The New World has not provided us with many things to do around here, aside from putting up a carnival that was secretly meant to kill half of us.

If people aren't reading, working, or in school, they are most likely talking about one of the ten TV shows that play on rotation. Devin and I don't like watching those shows because they are very predictable and don't make for a fun game.

One show called Criminals is about a married couple who just so happen to also be detectives. Each episode starts off with the couple finding out that there is some kind of criminal in the town that they live in, and they must stop them by finding evidence that leads them to the criminal or suspect. The couple always gets the criminal within the show's last few minutes, making it predictable, and Devin and I can't stand it.

Devin has more friends than I ever did because he's just a social butterfly. He can talk to anyone about anything. I am pretty sure he has talked to everyone in this town at some point in his life. Hell, I think he has even had a conversation with a tree about the soil it lives in.

I am more introverted, and when I was in school, I liked to play made up games with myself in class. Whenever I saw two people talking to each other, I would make up fake conversations for them just to make my day more enjoyable. My English teacher always said that I had a large and wild imagination.

I never minded not having friends because I had my family, but now, looking at our situation, I wish I would have gotten to know more about these people here. Or maybe not. If I were to know more people who came here tonight, then perhaps I would leave here even more brokenhearted if I knew they were going to be killed.

Aiden takes a second before speaking, "No. If it were Theon's group, there would be more than just three shots fired." This calms me down a little bit, but just because those shots were not for Theon's group, doesn't mean they weren't for another innocent person.

I can't believe these thoughts that are in my head. Thinking about another innocent person being shot at is not something I have ever done before. When we learned about the war with the Fritts, I always thought of the people who died in the same way I thought about a book character, they just weren't real. It is insensitive to think about those people who died and fought for us as fake, but it just made school easier. I probably should have taken school more seriously.

As we sit in silence, I think about our situation a little bit more. I have experienced guns, blood, and death, all in one day. This is similar to a war. We are in a war.

No, this can't be a war. Wars are fought by two sides with weapons. This is a slaughter. They didn't even give us a fighting chance. They have guns, and we have nothing but our hands. They have the security of the government and their soldiers, while we have mistrust and betrayal. We have no security. We don't even know if we can make it out of here alive tonight.

The worst part is we didn't even know this was going to happen to us. The government had us trusting them all this time. Meanwhile, they have been secretly planning on killing us for two years.

If the government had told us of the situation at the same time they found out, then maybe we could have come up with something better. The more brains, the more solutions, right? It makes me think that the government never had our best interests in mind and only looked out for themselves. Did they test their own intelligence and strength? I bet they didn't. If they had, they would have failed because they are idiots.

The Governors chose to kill the lives of innocents, and the best part is, they themselves didn't even have to get their hands dirty. They sent their guards, or shooters as Aiden and Theon called them, to do their dirty work.

Mass murder is not the solution to food and supply shortages. It can't be, it can never be. Is there something else they are not telling us about? Are we missing something? They have kept us secluded in our towns for years. What if there is something they don't want us to know about on the other side? What does the rest of the world really look like?

I have questioned these things before, but I never really lost sleep over them because I felt safe. I felt like I could trust our three Governors. I believed what they told me because they never gave me a reason not to.

They told us the rest of the world was a wasteland of destruction, that nothing was beyond our borders besides the remnants of past wars and battles. I always felt like I should not question these things since they provided us with a great life, didn't they?

"Time to go," Aiden stands and waits at the door for us. "Remember, stay close together in the shadows and be as quiet as possible."

When we all nod in agreement, he opens the door, cheeks to make sure it's clear, then steps outside. Since I am now the closest one to the door, I am the next person to leave the kitchen. Devin follows after me and then the three other people behind him.

I am now standing between my brother and Aiden, and I feel like a kid. The two of them are taller than me, and I'm not even that short. The two of them are just trees. Unlike my brother, Aiden seems to be a little older than me, probably in his early twenties, while Devin is only sixteen and will probably still grow a little more. I hope he doesn't.

We walk in the shadows for a few feet until we come to the end of the dark pathway. Before us now is the Ferris wheel to the left and a few other games in front of us across a somewhat medium size open area. Everything is still lit up, which is going to make it harder for us to sneak around to the maze.

Aiden looks at the area before him for a minute before turning back to us, "Okay listen, we are going to go one at a time across to the other side. Do you see the game lit up in blue? And the one lit up in green? We're going to run and hide in between those two games."

I see what he is talking about, but it's kind of far, and the only way to get there is by going through the wide open and well lit up area where anyone can see us. There is a small booth in the middle, but there is no way all of us can fit in there. I don't even think three of us would fit in it, and that's assuming we make it that far without getting shot.

"We are going to go one at a time. I will go first, then wave one of you guys over." He looks to us to make sure we understand before continuing, "Do what I do, watch my signals, and we will be fine."

Aiden waits until no one objects before making his move. He checks to ensure no shooters are coming, then runs midway across, stopping at the booth just before the Ferris wheel.

For the short time he is in the light, I can see that his dark hair is a mess. He has a little dirt on his face, but for some reason, he manages to look good. His shoes appear to be worn out but it doesn't seem to phase him.

He ducks down at the booth and waits a few seconds, checking again for any guards before running across the rest of the way to hide in between the darkness of two games. The whole time he is out there, he never once stands up straight. He always stays crouched down and keeps his knees bent.

He comes out of the darkness just enough for us to see him, and then he looks around again before waving us over.

We all look at each other, wondering who should go next. No one wants to be the first to go, but we all will eventually have to run to the other side if we're going to get out of here.

Chapter 11

A guy speaks up, "I will go first if none of you want to." There is no objection to his decision, so he walks out of the darkness, makes his way over to the other side, and stops midway as Aiden did.

When he enters the light, I can see that the guy is about thirty years old. The guy looks vaguely familiar. I think he works at the clothing store or department store or something like that. I just know that I have seen him before, but I don't know who he is. He has what looks like some blood on his shirt, but it does not look like he has any injuries on him, so I try not to think about where the blood came from.

His movements are not as stealthy as Aiden's, so when he runs, the sound of his shoes hitting the ground echoes through the night. I wince at this and hope it won't alert anyone. He navigates his way between the two games where Aiden is hiding, and Aiden puts his hand, signaling us to wait.

Aiden peeks out from behind the booths, his eyes scanning the area before he retreats back into the shadows. About ten seconds later, the silence is broken by the sound of heavy footsteps coming our way. I exchange a worried glance with Devin, fearing that the guard will find us.

Devin's expression matches mine, along with the other two people we are with. We all quickly move further back so that we are more hidden in the darkness. I see three guards walking by quickly, and I let out a sigh of relief when none of them look our way and instead just keep walking.

I make my way back over to the edge of where we are standing, and I look for Aiden. I see Aiden peeking his head out from behind the games on the other side once again, and I assume he sees nothing because he then waves the next person over.

Some girl goes next, followed by the younger girl, who I assume is the same girl who was concerned for Theon's group when the gunshots were heard. When the young girl runs across, I can see that she looks to be twelve or thirteen, and I once again can't help but think she's too young to experience something like this.

She was probably having a great day with her parents, possibly siblings, and friends when the government came and destroyed her outlook on life. I think about the fantastic night my Dad, Devin, and I were having before going to that stupid surprise. We should have just ignored this whole event, but we were in such desperate need for entertainment and fun.

After she makes it to the other side, Devin and I are the only ones left hiding in the dark pathway. I don't want Devin to be left alone, so I suggest he go first. He looks concerned with my decision but does it anyway.

I don't know if our Dad survived the shooters, and I have no idea what they did to the people who didn't show up to the carnival like my mom. All I know is that Devin is the only family member that I know is alive and well right now, and I can't let anything bad happen to him.

I watch Devin as he goes across. He looks around as he makes his way to the booth midway. Each step he takes is cautious. He bends down a little as he walks, but I can tell he's not comfortable doing this.

When he eventually makes it to the other side with the others, I am able to relax, knowing that he is alright, but I get tense again when Aiden waves me over.

I take a moment to breathe and look around before quickly moving toward the same booth everyone else stopped at. I am hyperaware of the lights on me, and I try turning them off with my mind. Obviously, that doesn't work.

I try taking small, light steps in hopes of remaining quiet, and I think this works. I am about to reach the booth in the center, but I catch the sight of a tall, moving figure out of the corner of my eye. I only get a quick glance, but I think the person is dressed in a dark uniform and is walking by the Ferris wheel, which just so happens to be only a few feet away from me.

My fight or flight instinct kicks in, and I quickly run into the booth and get down lower to try to hide myself as well as I can. I am not about to find out if I am a good fighter or not, at least not today.

I sit down and close my eyes, waiting to hear the sound of a gunshot. Stupid Sam, now you are going to die. You should have looked more thoroughly before crossing. I wait another minute, but nothing happens.

I slowly reopen my eyes and look around. The guard is only a few feet away from me, but he doesn't seem to see me. I quickly scoot further into the booth, hoping he doesn't look my way.

I look over to Aiden, who is just visible in the darkness. He looks at me and puts up a hand to tell me to stay where I am. Then he disappears into the darkness again. I catch the sight of Devin, and he looks worried, but when he catches me looking at him, he gives me a weak, encouraging smile.

When Aiden comes back out of the darkness, he has something in his hand that is too small for me to tell what it is. He looks to the guard, who is facing away from him, and he throws whatever he has in his hand in the direction the guard came from.

The guard immediately pulls out his gun and runs over to the noise. I look back at Aiden and see him waving me over to the group. I run as fast as I can over to them. I think I am going to have a heart attack because of how fast my heart is racing. I look back to see that the guard is gone, and I relax. "Thank you," I say to Aiden.

"No problem."

Devin hugs me but doesn't say anything as Aiden leads us behind a row of game booths. It's dark behind the booths, but there is still about a foot and a half of light separating one game from another. Along with that, there are also many wires, so we all have to be careful.

We all slowly and carefully step around the wires and do our best not to get stuck in them. The young girl in front of Devin and me almost trips a couple of times, but luckily, we only have to catch her from falling once. The girl is young, and I can tell she's scared. I understand what she's feeling, so I hold her hand until we get to the end, where there are no more games to hide behind.

In front of us now is another open area, but this one is not as big as the last or as brightly lit up. Across the way is our destination, the mirror maze. I give the young girl's hand a small squeeze to let her know that we are almost out of this nightmare.

Instead of running to the other side like last time, Aiden leads us through a series of dark spots to get there. There are some gunshots heard in the distance, and the girl holds my hand tighter. I look around, but I don't see anyone. The area around us is hauntingly quiet and dark.

We reach the mirror maze, but Aiden takes us through the exit door instead of going in through the entrance.

Once inside, Aiden addresses the group, "Stay close so no one gets lost. Hold hands if you have to."

I take Devin's hand with my free one, and we follow Aiden through the maze. The maze is still lit up, and I can't help but stare at myself in the reflection as we walk. The bright light around the mirror gives me the unfortunate ability to see myself very clearly.

My shirt has some spots of dirt on it, and my jeans have a hole in the knee that was not there before. I have loose strands of hair sticking out in weird directions from my head, and my face looks different somehow. It is like today's events have taken away some of the liveliness in my features.

My eyes do not seem as bright, and my mouth doesn't hold a smile. I thought I lost the feeling of a kid when I grew up, graduated school, and got a job, but now I know that that's not true. I still had some child-like tendencies and thoughts, but not anymore. They took whatever part of me that was still a kid that was left in me.

I look beside me at Devin, who has a leaf stuck in his hair. He looks tired, sad, and drained of all the joy he had earlier today. I look at the rest of the group and see that we all look to be in the same condition, beaten and tired.

Aiden stops in a corner of the maze, and we all watch as he pushes one of the mirrors, which swings open like a door.

The other side of the door is dark but I can just make out the trees of Treegrass in the distance. Now that we're here, I have no idea what to do. We are supposed to go out the door and do what exactly? Run from the government? Join the Jumpers? Go home?

Then another thought occurs to me. What if my Dad is still inside the carnival, and we are leaving without him?

Aiden steps out the door and then turns around to look at us after we don't follow, "Are you coming or what?"

Chapter 12

Is freedom from this terrible night really only a few feet away?

I guess I'm not the only one who thinks this since everyone stares at Aiden for a good long minute before slowly and skeptically walking out the door one by one.

When I step out the door, it takes my eyes a second to adjust to the darkness of the outside world. From the looks of it, the brightly lit carnival looks like the safe place to be, and Treegrass is dangerous, but looks can be deceiving.

The town is engulfed by darkness, with only minimal lights on in the houses around the carnival. The distant trees, whose branches are almost bare in this early spring, stand ominously against the night sky. The carnival, once emitting a bright, joyous light, now seems like a distant bad memory. Its look of safety and excitement is a mere illusion.

I remember when we were kids, Devin and I would join the other kids in exploring the woods. We would run through the trees and make up stories about how a witch might live inside the biggest tree in the woods. We would spend all day searching for the biggest tree and then arguing about which was really bigger.

Over the course of a few months, we would grow tired of the same stupid fights and stories, and then slowly, people would stop coming to the woods because there was simply nothing more to do. Devin and I stopped going for a while because there was nothing interesting to do there by ourselves, and we had exhausted every game we could think of. But one night, the power went out, and we saw a group of younger kids running into the woods.

Of course, Devin and I were not about to miss the great opportunity to scare the crap out of some random kids. So we grabbed rakes and anything else made of metal that we could find, and then we ran into the woods, dragging them behind us and hitting them together and on trees to scare the kids. The look on the kids' faces, along with their high-pitched screams, were hilarious, and no one would go into the woods at night by our house again unless they were dared to.

Aiden closes the door of the mirror maze, cutting off the little light we had. We all stand right outside the carnival. Houses are only a few hundred feet from us, and I wonder if the people living in these houses heard any of the gunshots or if they all went into the carnival. Aiden starts walking towards the trees in the distance, and we all follow him.

I am still uncertain about Aiden and the people he refers to as the Jumpers. I really don't know much about these people other than what Aiden had said about them. How do we know they aren't just as dangerous and misleading as the New World government? Could this all be an elaborate trap?

We are strangers to the people in these other distant towns. How do we really know they are who they said they are? What if they are trying to steal from us like the Fritts did in the past?

With all of this in mind, I keep my hold on Devin's hand along with the hand of the younger girl whom I have never met before tonight. While I may not know this girl personally, I feel like I have to protect her from any more bad things that could happen, at least until we figure out what we are going to do next.

As we get closer to the tree line closest to our town border, I wonder where Aiden plans to take us. We can't get past the border—at least, I don't think we can. None of us have ever tried before. But then again, Aiden and the rest of the Jumpers got in here, so there must be a way.

Even if we can get past the border, then what? We leave all our belongings behind and live in no man's land? We don't even know for sure what lies beyond the border. We only know what we have been told, and it isn't much.

"Where are we going?" I ask.

Aiden speaks without looking back at me, "Theon and the others brought the groups of people they got out of the carnival to the border of your town, where they will be hidden in the trees."

I can't help but wonder if my Dad made it into one of those groups and is waiting for us. I want to run to where Aiden is talking about just so I can see my Dad again, but I know there is a good chance I would get lost, and I shouldn't get my hopes up that he will be there.

My Dad might be dead, but I have to keep a positive attitude on the matter until I know for sure. After I know for certain about my

Dad, I will find out about my Mother. Maybe she is safe from the shooters since she did not attend the carnival.

The people who didn't come here tonight would have to have heard all the shooting and yelling coming from the carnival, at least the people in the houses nearby, right?

"What about the people who didn't go to the carnival? What did they do with them? Are they safe?" I ask Aiden.

Aiden gives me a quick glance but doesn't say anything.

"What do they do with them?" I ask again because I have to know if my Mother is alright.

Aiden seems like he doesn't want to answer this question, but I don't care.

"From what I heard from some of our townspeople we snuck out of Tundris following the carnival, the officials send someone to go door to door. We don't know for sure what happens after that. Some people who were fleeing the carnival say they heard gunshots coming from inside some of the houses while others say that they heard absolutely nothing."

Aiden continues, "Only one guy I know said that he didn't go to the carnival and that he was sitting at home when he got a knock on his door. When he answered it there was a guard who asked to come in. He let the guard in since guards arriving at your house aren't supposed to mean anything bad."

He is right. It is not common for a guard to show up at a person's house, but when they do, there is usually no reason not to invite them in. They do general sweeps of a home if they are trying to find something that was stolen and other times, they are just doing a general wellness check.

Aiden stops for a second before speaking again. "He said that the guard asked him why he didn't go to the carnival. He thought nothing of it and told the guard that he recently lost his daughter a few months ago due to the harsh winter, and he didn't want to see other kids and be reminded of the one he lost. He said the guard seemed nice up until there was a commotion outside."

"What happened?" I ask.

"He said that while the guard didn't seem to have a gun, he still didn't feel safe since the guard wouldn't let him get up to look outside. He said as the sound got louder, the guard became more agitated. At that moment, the guy pushed the guard out of the way and started running out of his house. That's when he said he saw the carnival and heard the people screaming. He later managed to find our group, and together, we all fled Tundris and started trying to figure out what to do next. We don't know for certain if the guard was going to kill him, but my guess is that he would have."

As we walk closer to the trees, the group remains silent, and I try to think of anything else besides my Mother's possible fate. It doesn't work. Did someone really show up at our house to kill her after we left?

"Why would they do that? Why kill the people who didn't even get a chance to score any points and save themselves?" Devin asks.

"I don't know," Aiden says, "But if I had to guess, it would be because the people who didn't show up to the carnival were seen as not wanting to participate in the government's game. They probably saw them as a threat or as uncooperative and killed them."

I decide to stop asking questions and let what he told me sink in. The more I think about it, the sicker I feel, and I can't help but feel so stupid. I really thought we were safe and that we could trust them. We are supposed to trust them.

As we walk, I think about how dangerous what we are doing is. If one guard decides to shine a flashlight out here, then they will definitely see us and tell all the other guards. With each snap of a twig or crunch of a leaf, my heart skips a beat. I can't help but think we have to be as quiet as possible so that no one hears us.

When the sound of us walking into the group of trees becomes too much for me to handle, I can't help but ask Aiden, "Won't the guards hear or see us out here? Is this safe?"

Aiden doesn't stop walking when he answers, "No, from what we have seen, the shooters don't leave the carnival until the morning. Our theory is that they think they have everyone trapped inside, so there is no need to look outside. We believe the ones that go into the townspeople's homes who didn't go to the carnival stay inside the person's home or at least a given street to stay at until the morning comes. That's what we think, anyway. We haven't seen any out here."

He takes a quick glance at me and then says, "We'll be fine. We're covered in darkness, so they can't see us anyway."

That's a reasonable response, but I still can't help but feel like they will come looking for us and find us easily. Devin must sense my unease because he squeezes my hand and tries to give me a reassuring smile.

After a few more minutes of walking, I start hearing hushed voices in the distance. As we get closer, I can see that it's a group of about thirty to forty Treegrass people. They are all standing around in an opening between the trees, talking among themselves.

The young girl whose hand I have been holding lets go and runs at the group of people before stopping to hug someone. I assume she must have found a family member or friend.

Other people start walking around looking for familiar faces, and I find myself doing the same. I drag Devin with me as I try to see if our Dad is out here somewhere.

If other people can find their loved ones out here, then so can I. It's really dark, so I try to get close to people to see if Dad is out here anywhere. I look from one person to another, moving around in circles. Some people look back at me like I'm crazy. Others look like they see right through me. I sometimes think I caught a glance of him, but when I look closer, it is always some other guy. Why does every middle aged guy have to look so similar to one another?

I swear they do it on purpose. Everyone my Dad's age has a similar haircut, similar T-shirts, the same jeans, and the same stupid jokes. No one is making any jokes out here, but I know that if the situation were different and I was talking to these guys, then they would quickly say something stupid that would make me laugh.

I don't see him. I make my way around again to make sure. Maybe I missed him. Most people are standing around, but a few are sitting on fallen trees or on the ground. I lower myself to look at the faces of the people sitting down, but no one looks familiar. I try walking around and calling for my Dad without being too loud, but I get no answer. I go around another time to see if I missed him, but I don't think I did.

He's not here.

Chapter 13

Devin pulls me in for a hug, and I tell him what I know he can see, "He's not here."

Devin holds me tighter, "I know."

"He's not here," I say once again, more to myself than to Devin. The person who helped raise us and taught us everything in life is gone, and we never got to say goodbye. A wave of sadness washes over me, and I have to fight to hold back tears. After another moment, I start to feel anger build up inside of my chest.

No. I tell myself. He's not dead, he's just not here.

We survived, we made it out. Maybe he's alive too. And even better, maybe he is unharmed. It is unlikely but not impossible. Maybe he is still in there looking for a way out. Maybe he has been looking for us in there this whole time, and we left without him.

These thoughts flood my mind as I stand here. I think of all the possible places he could be and all the ways that he could have gotten away from those guards he tackled.

I hope he is uninjured, but my Dad against two guards is not the safest of situations, and if he is alive, then it is safe to assume that he is injured in some way. If he is injured, then he probably needs help getting out.

I push away from Devin and look around the group of people again until I find Aiden. Aiden is standing to the side, talking to another guy who I don't think I have seen before. By the looks of his dirty, torn clothes, he's a Jumper like Aiden.

They are in the middle of a conversation as I walk up to them.

"I want to go back in," I stay. I eye the two of them down, silently daring one of them to try and stop me.

The two of them stop their conversation and look at me like I'm crazy. "Excuse me?" Aiden asks, lifting one of his eyebrows in question.

"I want to go back into the carnival," I state once again, but this time, I make it clear that it's not a question. There will be no changing my mind. I look at them deadpanned. The anger in me I felt before is still present, and there is no masking it. "I just want someone to bring me back into the carnival so I can look for my Dad. You can wait by the maze, you don't even have to go in. I can go alone, but I do need someone to show me how to get back there."

The guy who Aiden was talking to looks at me like I have two heads before he changes his expression to one of sympathy. "Look, sweaty," I raise my eyebrows so high I think they reach the moon. "The odds of your Dad still being alive are slim, and I don't want you risking your life or any of our lives just for you to go looking for a dead man," he says.

I don't know who this guy thinks he is talking to, but I am not a kid, nor am I stupid. I know this isn't a good idea, but I just want to find my father. He is my family. I have to try anything I can to bring him back if he is still alive in there.

I am about to give this guy a mouthful of my mind, but Aiden puts his hand up, stopping me before I get to say anything.

"While I don't agree with the manner in which my friend said that," Aiden pauses to give a quick glare at his so-called friend. "I do agree that it's best if we all stay together. We got everyone we could find out, and now it is too risky to go back in when there will be shooters walking all around in there. I understand that many of you guys still have family in there, and they might still be in the show tent, but there is no way we can get them out safely. We can't have everyone go in looking for their loved ones, that just wouldn't end well. Someone would be bound to lead the shooters back here, and we can't compromise the lives of everyone here. I'm sorry."

"You guys compromised your own lives to go in there and bring us out. Why can't we go back in? There could still be more people in there needing someone to help them get out," I tell them.

"That was different. The more times people go in and out of the carnival through the maze, the greater the chance of one of the shooters figuring out that is what we are using, and they will figure it out and follow us out here. It is too risky to keep going in and out of the carnival. No," Aiden says.

I argue back, "I am not asking to keep going in and out of the carnival. I am just asking to go back in once. Like I said, you don't even have to go with me once we are inside, so let me go."

"If you go, then more people will want to go, and then the next thing you know, there will be a flow of people going in and out of the carnival through the maze. So no," Aiden says with more authority.

I am so angry that I can barely get my thoughts straight to speak. "Fine, I will find the way there myself," I state and then walk away from the two of them. I make my way in a random direction, hoping it is the right one.

I know that I am not necessarily mad at them, rather, I'm mad at the situation, but I can't help it. I want to march up to where the government is located in the town of Officials and scream my head off, maybe even punch some people, but I know that it is not possible, and it would be a suicide mission.

So instead, I make my way through the trees, trying to find a way back to the carnival, but it's hard since everything is so dark. It also does not help that I have a tendency to get lost easily in the woods. I try not to make that known to too many people, especially Devin.

It feels surreal that just a few hours ago, I was making fun of Devin for having no directional skills, yet I have no idea where I'm going. I am usually good at navigating my way through the town since I have lived here my whole life, but the woods are a whole other thing. It also does not help that tonight's events have messed with my mind. I am having a harder time than usual trying to figure out where I am and where I am going.

I make it to the tree line before he catches up to me. "Sam, stop," Devin says behind me, but I don't listen. "Sam! Stop!" He whispers yells and grabs my arm.

I turn around to face him, "He can still be alive, Devin."

"I know," he looks down before looking back at me, "The likelihood of him being alive is slim. While there is a small chance he is still alive, there is a hundred percent chance that you are still alive, and I would like to keep it that way. You're the only family I have right now. I can't lose you."

The look on his face tells me that what I'm doing is selfish. Here I am, wanting to risk my life to find our Dad, but Devin is standing in front of me, tired and defeated, asking me not to. If something bad happens to me in there, then he will be left with no one. I should take what I have as a good thing and not go looking for things that I want.

But I really want to find my Dad.

"I just really need to know what happened to him. If he's okay," I say, trying to fight the tears that I feel forming in my eyes.

"I know," Devin tells me.

I am tired. I can't go back into the carnival by myself, it's too dangerous. I probably wouldn't even make it out of the maze. I look back at Devin for a minute, and then give him a small nod of agreement.

I wipe my eyes and the two of us start walking back through the trees to the others in silence. We walk with a few feet of distance between us. I don't know if Devin knows how to get back to the group, but I know that I don't have a clue. In the daytime, I could probably find my way around here pretty quickly, but since it's so dark and my brain is clouded by today's events, everything just looks the same.

"Giving up so quickly? I thought for sure you would be at the door to the maze by now."

Devin and I both look up to see Aiden standing by a tree, looking at the two of us.

"You said I couldn't go, so I'm not going," I say reluctantly. He is not the real reason I'm not going, Devin is, but he doesn't need to know that. If I pretend that I am listening to him and doing as he says, then maybe I will gain some trust with him. If he turns out to be no better than the New World, then I can use this trust to my advantage.

Aiden nods in remembrance, "Yeah, well, I changed my mind, but if you don't want to go, then you can stay here with the others," Aiden says and starts walking past us toward the direction Devin and I were coming from.

I lift my head up skeptically, "What made you change your mind? I thought going back in was too dangerous."

He stops and turns to the two of us. "Well, it turns out one of the Jumpers, Vesper, found a room with a list of where the government plans on taking the carnival next. He was only able to write down a few of the names before hearing a shooter coming. I plan on getting the rest of the names along with where the towns might be located."

Aiden looks at me, "He told me the room was over by the big tent where they had the show, and I figured that if you wanted to, you could come with me and look for your Dad along the way."

The offer is tempting, but I told Devin I wouldn't go. I look over to Devin with pleading eyes, and he looks back at me deep in thought.

Devin's eyes tell me no, but after a few more seconds of me silently pleading with him, he turns back to Aiden and says, "She can go only if you promise to keep her safe."

"Of course," Aiden says with a nod of respect.

I hug Devin and thank him a million times. "Just come back in one piece, okay?" He says to me.

I reassure Devin that I will be fine before turning back to Aiden. Aiden starts walking through the woods once more, and I glance back at Devin to give him a reassuring smile before following Aiden.

We walk for a few minutes in the trees before reaching the tree line. I can see a little bit of light shining out from where the carnival is straight ahead of us. It turns out I was half right in the direction I was walking in before.

Aiden holds his hand up for a moment and stops. "Just to be clear, we have about five to six hours before the sun comes up. When that happens, that group back there," Aiden points in the direction in which we came, "will have to leave. The shooters will come into the town, so it will be too dangerous to stay. Hopefully, we will be out and back with them long before that happens. Move fast and stay close, understand?"

"Yes."

"Good."

With that, Aiden moves towards the direction of the maze, and I follow. Maybe I'm stupid for going back in, but I need to know for sure if he is alive or not, even if that means risking my life.

Chapter 14

Aiden and I walk across the open area to the maze, neither of us saying anything. I am starting to notice that despite our situation, not many people have much to say tonight. I guess there really isn't much to say about your own government trying to kill you.

I wonder what Devin is doing with the others back in the trees. Is he socializing with them like he usually does with strangers, or is he sitting alone waiting for me? I hope it is the first option.

If I do not come back, then Devin might not have any more family. I should not think about that right now. I need to keep focused on what is happening rather than what could happen.

"You said you were from Tundris?" I ask Aiden, hoping that this will distract me from worrying about my brother.

All he says is, "Yeah," I wait for him to elaborate more and start telling me about Tundris, but he doesn't.

"What was it like there? Are there really big snow storms there like we see on the news?" Aiden looks at me like it's an odd question to ask, but it seems pretty normal to me.

"Yeah, Tundris has really long winters and short summers." After another moment, he adds, "I like it better where we are now."

"So, you hate the snow?" I ask, but he doesn't answer, "Why? The news always shows kids playing in the snow, isn't it supposed to be fun? Don't you guys have snowball fights, build snowmen, and do things like that?"

Aiden seems a little annoyed by this question, and I regret bringing up the topic of his old town. It's probably hard talking about a home you can never return to. I don't even know if he has his parents. Did the shooters kill them? Are they back at the Jumpers camp? I don't ask.

"I'm sorry. I shouldn't have asked."

After a few more minutes go by, Aiden finally talks again. "Kids playing in the snow, is that what they showed you?" Aiden says, sounding a little belligerent. "Did they also show the roofs that collapsed on people because their houses were not built properly to hold that much snow? Did they tell you about the people who froze because the government wanted to preserve as much energy as possible by limiting the amount of electricity we got? How little heat we got."

Aiden looks at me, "No, of course they wouldn't show you that." Aiden scoffs, "The New World really is a piece of shit."

Aiden keeps going, "I thought that the carnival was going to be the government's way of saying sorry for all their poor choices, but instead, they made the worst decision they ever could have made. I hope to one day make them regret it."

I don't know what to say. How could I have been so naïve to believe that each town lived good lives like we do here in Treegrass? I thought the whole point of the New World was that everyone is safe here, we have food, resources, and protection, or at least we did, didn't we?

"Sorry," is all I say, but I know it does nothing.

"Don't be sorry. You are not the one who failed us. Our government should be the one saying sorry."

We walk in silence for the remainder of the time it takes us to reach the maze. Aiden puts his hand on the door but waits to open it. "Ready?" he asks. I nod my head in response, and Aiden opens the door.

When I step in, I wince at the bright lights. When my eyes adjust again, I see that my reflection, along with Aiden's, can be seen all around us. Aiden moves swiftly, making a series of turns around the maze. He looks down while he does this, making me think he uses the same technique that I once did.

We come to the exit door and quickly look at one another before Aiden slowly cracks the door open. He peaks out of the opening of the door and then opens it wider to step out.

I think that coming back in here would probably make me an idiot, but I tell myself that this is like a game. Aiden and I are just playing a game of hide and seek, except in this game, when you are found, you die. Fun.

Just like before, the area outside the maze is poorly lit and quiet. There is no one around, so Aiden leads us back over the path behind all the games.

We go behind the games, and I carefully walk around the wires to make sure I don't trip. Just like before, there is a foot of open space between where we are and the next game, and that space is brighter than the area behind the games. I cross the space with one stride, but something on the ground catches my eye. I look back to the ground and see that it's blood.

Someone was either injured or killed here.

"Don't look at it," Aiden says, putting his arm on my shoulder to steer me away from the site.

I wonder whose it is. Is it a stranger's, or could it possibly be my Dad's? I feel like a terrible person for hoping that it belongs to a stranger.

Why couldn't this day just be what it was advertised to be?

I wish I were back sitting under the big tent watching the show. At the end, they would announce the top three winners of the games, as Devin had predicted, and then we would go home and tell our Mom all about it.

There would be no bad news, no betrayal, no death.

I come back to reality when we reach the end of the pathway. The Ferris wheel is right before us. The lights are still on, but like before, the ride is not moving. It is in the same spot that we had to cross over from the kitchen to get to.

If the New World was having serious food and supply shortages, then how did they find the supplies to do all of this? And where are all the people who ran the games? I have not seen a single one of them since walking into the show.

Most of the people running the games were women, yet I do not recall seeing a single female guard. Do the workers know what happens at the carnival? Where do they come from? Are they from another town that has yet to be targeted by the government, or are they from the town of Officials? If they are from the town of Officials, then they probably know what has been going on.

All government officials live in their own town, which is located in an old city that has been rebuilt just for them. Each town has its own small police force, but they are rarely needed. The majority of the New World's essential people, along with the military, are located within the town of Officials.

"Okay, we are not going to go back that way. Vesper said to keep going straight. The room he found was over by the rock wall and the big show tent." Aiden whispers, "If your Dad's alive, then he will most likely be with the other green box people in that tent."

I look down. "My Dad threw the games for my brother and me... he had a red light on his box."

Aiden looks apologetic and looks thoughtful for a minute before speaking again. "Did he make it out of the tent with you?"

"Yeah, he helped knock the fence over."

"Then maybe he's still out here somewhere hiding from the shooters," Aiden says, giving me a small reassuring smile.

I tell myself that what he says is true and that my Dad is hiding behind one of the games. I know the likelihood of this happening is slim, but I can't give up on him. He never gave up on us.

I give Aiden a small smile and nod to tell him that he's right, "So, how do we get to that room?"

"Just follow me. We'll stop at some of the stands on the way and see if anyone is in them. Maybe your Dad is hiding out there."

I nod in understanding, and then Aiden continues, "Stick by me and do what I do. If we somehow get separated, then try to meet back at the kitchen where Theon brought you earlier."

"Okay," I say, and then Aiden peers out of the darkness to check if the coast is clear.

Instead of leading us across to the kitchen where we came from before, Aiden walks to the left, going behind the stands that all seem to be lined up against a wall. There is still enough space for us to move behind them but it is smaller than the normal booths.

If my memory serves me right, we should be over by the food court, and these stands probably gave out the food. Aiden emerges from the shadows, moving into the booth from the open side. He comes back out a second later, his head shaking no. There is no one inside.

He continues to do this for the remainder of the food booths, and then they turn back into the regular game booths. Each step he takes is a careful one, and I can tell by his eye movements that he is perceptive about everything he sees. The game booths, still illuminated, force us to remain hidden as best as we can.

We both make sure to stay in as much darkness as possible while still being able to see our surroundings before moving on to the next booth. Aiden checks to make sure no one is coming before he sneaks into the next stand and then the next. No one is in either one of them.

Aiden comes back to join me behind the next game booth, and we both freeze as the sound of heavy boots reverberates from the other side of the stand. Each step I hear echoes in my head, reminding me of how risky this is.

I look at Aiden, and he puts a finger over his mouth to tell me to be quiet. The two of us stand there in silence, staring at each other.

CHAPTER 15

The footsteps stop only a few feet away from us, so the guard must have stopped for something. Does he know we're behind here? Why is he just standing there? The suspense is killing me. Am I going to be shot any second or not?

Another minute goes by, and footsteps are heard walking off. I close my eyes in relief before reopening them. I peer out the right side of the stand and see the guard walking off in the distance. I can tell right away that if he were to have seen us, then we would definitely be dead. That guard is huge, even if he didn't have a gun I think he could still kill us without breaking a sweat.

Just by looking at his back, I can see that the guard would be a force to be wrecked with. He has big arms and is very tall. He could probably knock me out just by flicking me. I am glad that he didn't see Aiden or me here. If he had, we would not have been able to fight or run from him. That guy is built like a tank.

Aiden and I stay behind the booth for another minute just to make sure no one else is coming, then we cross to the next game booth. Aiden looks inside, but once again, no one is in there. This game is the last in the line of games, and Aiden looks out from behind the booth once more before motioning with his head to follow him.

He steps out from behind the game and leads us a few feet away to a tree. Once there, I see that there is an opening in the fence that is used as a doorway. Aiden walks up to it, cautiously looks at the other side, and then enters it. I follow him and try to stay as close as possible. He seems to know what he is doing, and I don't want to get separated from him.

This is a smaller game area that is a little more secluded from the other part of the carnival, but I remember playing the games over here with Devin and our Dad. Aiden goes into the games like before to check if anyone is in them, but once again, they are all empty.

It's disappointing to think that there is no one out here anymore. They have either been taken back to the tent or killed.

As Aiden moves through more booths and some smaller stands, I start silently wishing for him to find anyone, not just my father. The small group of people back in the trees outside the carnival, along with half the population the guards did not kill, can't really be the only people left alive. There have to be others out here somewhere. We just have to find them.

As we are walking, I sometimes catch the sight of blood on the ground. I try to ignore it, but it's hard. We turn a corner where more games are lined up against the draped fence, and I can see the rock wall in the distance. It's tall, lit up and red, very red. I don't know what happened there, but I am glad I didn't have to witness it. The amount of blood dripping down from the top to the bottom is enough to make me want to throw up.

Who died here? Were they killed because they had a red light on their box or because they escaped the big show tent?

I don't think I'll ever know because, from the looks of it, the guards must be taking away the bodies as they kill them. In all the places there is blood, there are no bodies. Maybe people were shot and then got away, or perhaps the bullet was fatal.

We move through the game booths, clearing them to ensure no one is in them and then moving on to the next. These game booths are closer to the big tent where we had the show, and there are more guards over here than anywhere else we have been tonight. Aiden and I make sure to be extra careful to stay as far back from the light as we can.

We duck when we see guards coming our way, and we wait for them to pass before moving on. Some of the guards I see are just simply walking around casually as if they didn't just kill the lives of innocent people. Others seem to be walking around holding papers as if they are someone important.

We pass the rock wall and get behind the last booth at the end. We don't check to see if anyone is inside since there are too many guards moving around. There is a little bit of fabric hanging off the edge of the booth, so Aiden and I use it to hide ourselves better.

Across from us is the big tent where the horror of the night started. There seems to be no one going in or out of the tent, but there are about four guards standing at the entrance to it, each one holding a big gun.

The only time I had ever seen someone holding a gun that big was when we watched videos of the war. Each man in those videos always had a big gun that was able to fire off many shots at once, effectively shooting many people at once. It scares me to think that the government is treating this situation like a war against its own people.

"There are two small buildings by the tent. One of them must be the building that Vesper was talking about," Aiden says in a quiet whisper.

I look over, and sure enough, there are two small square buildings in front of the tent. One is more to the right, and the other is more to the left of where we are, they don't look like much, but then again, the government probably designed them that way so no one would take interest in them.

"We will first check the building on the left since it's the closest one. The only problem we'll have is getting past the guards."

"Can we cause a distraction like you did earlier when the shooter was by me? They seem to be interested in finding the people who got out." I tell Aiden.

Aiden seems to think about this for a moment. He looks around at all the guards and then at the games around him.

After a minute, he speaks again, "Okay, here's what we're going to do. I am going to go a few booths over and turn on one or two games. That should be enough reason for some of the shooters to head my way. When they do, you are going to run into the left building and check to see if what we are looking for is in there. If there is, write it down, if there isn't then check the other building."

Aiden takes a small notepad and pen out of his back pocket and hands it to me.

"We will meet back up in the kitchen. Do you remember how to get there from here?"

"Yes, but Aiden, I don't know what I really am supposed to be looking for. Why don't you get the information, and I'll turn the games on?" I really don't want to write down meaningless information and overlook the important stuff.

Aiden puts a hand on my shoulder, "I can outrun the shooters, and I promised that guy back in those trees that I would get you back safely. This is the best plan if I want to keep that promise."

I think about it for a moment. If Aiden sets off the games and the guards run in that direction, then I have a good chance of making it to the first room. The door is on the side facing us, not the guards by the main tent holding everyone in. If all goes well, then I get the information the Jumpers want, and then I meet Aiden in the kitchen.

"That guy is my brother." I don't know why I feel the need to make that clear, but for some reason, I do. "What information should I specifically be looking for?" I ask Aiden reluctantly.

He nods in approval, "Anything that looks important, but keep an eye out for anything that resembles a list of towns, maybe even a map if you can. If you have to steal the map, do it. The less time it takes you to get in and out, the better."

"Okay," I just have to find a list and any other possibly useful information if I can. It should be easy. Will it be easy? That is the real question.

"I am going to go now. You wait here until you see the shooters running towards the sound, then run."

I nod in understanding, and then Aiden turns to check to see if there are any guards walking by, but I stop him.

"Aiden," Aiden turns around and waits for me to speak. "Do you always keep your promises?"

"I try my best, why?"

"Can you promise me that you will be in the kitchen? I don't want to wait for someone who might never show up, and I also don't want to leave without you, so can you promise that you will be there?"

Aiden looks at me in the eyes, and with all seriousness, he says, "I promise to try my hardest to make it back to the room for you."

"Thank you," I really hope he is able to keep his promise because I am serious. I will not be leaving without him.

Aiden checks again to make sure the coast is clear before giving me one last glance, and then he leaves.

I watch as he moves around, hiding behind anything he can to ensure no guards see him. It's not until I can no longer see Aiden that I look away and I focus on my goal.

I wait in the dark and watch as some guards walk by me. I know they can't see me behind the booth, but it still makes me nervous to think that if I make one wrong move, then I could ruin the plan and possibly end up dead.

For the most part, the area is silent, but I can still hear the sound of people when they walk by. About five minutes go by, and I start to think that Aiden is in trouble because I hear nothing, and I start to panic.

What do I do if he doesn't set the game off? If I stay here, I would most certainly be found by the morning, and they would kill me.

I close my eyes and tell myself to stop thinking like that. If I want to succeed, I have to think about the positives, not the negatives. So, instead, I count how many seconds pass in my head to distract myself.

...Fifteen, sixteen, seventeen. Loud, fast music is heard in the distance, and I just know it's from Aiden. I open my eyes and stand up straighter.

It's time.

CHAPTER 16

I peek out from where I am hiding. There are three guards running in Aiden's direction, and one guard is left standing at the show tent's entrance.

I do not see anyone else around besides that one guard, but he is looking straight ahead, and the door to the first building is out of his eye range. I move out from behind the booth, and I quickly move to the first of the small buildings. I have no choice but to walk in the direct light, so if anyone were to walk by and look my way, I would be a goner.

I walk over to the door quickly and open it. Without thinking, I walk into the room and close the door behind me. I can feel the adrenaline coursing through my veins, acting as a reminder of how badly this can end up.

The room has a single light on, but it is enough for me to see everything. Once I look at my surroundings, I realize that I am an idiot for not checking to see if anyone was in the room first. Luckily, there is not, but the empty chairs around a square table tell me that there could have been.

On the table, there is a half-eaten sandwich that looks like someone abandoned it in a rush. That person can be coming back here any second. I have to move fast. I look around at the rest of the room. There is a smaller table on the back wall, and sitting on that table are about eight to ten black bags of various sizes.

I make my way over to the bags within three strides to make sure I don't waste any more time than I need to. I pick up the first bag on the end of the table and I look through its contents. After finding only a few pairs of clothes along with some food I move on to the next one. The following three bags seem to be similar to the first, meaning there is nothing worthwhile in them. I am starting to lose hope that this room, which was relatively easy to get to, is the right room.

I then move onto a medium sized black leather bag. I unzip the bag, and the first thing that catches my eye is a small, slick black flashlight. There are also some loose papers, but after giving them a quick look over, I determine that they don't contain anything of importance, so I put them back. The next thing I see is a notebook with literally no notes in it. I am starting to get frustrated. If there is nothing in this room that relates to what Vesper told Aiden, then I am wasting time looking in the wrong building.

I put the bag back down on the table, making a loud thunk when I do. At first, I think to myself, it was the flashlight, but then again, that noise sounded much heavier than the small flashlight that is in the bag. My heart races as I open the bag once again and take out the flashlight, papers, and notepad. I see a flap on the bottom of the bag blending in with the black fabric. I pull it back and see the cause of the noise. On the bottom of the bag, there is a small handgun.

I stare at the gun for a second before picking it up. The weapon is the darkest shade of black I have ever seen, and it lacks the shine that most metals have. The gun is cold to the touch and heavy in my hand. I have never held a gun before. For some reason, I thought it would feel different from holding a large piece of metal, but it does not. The way it fits in my hand makes it feel so real, so dangerous.

I am not quite sure what to do with it. Aiden didn't say anything about weapons. Should I bring it with me or leave it here? I have never shot a gun before, the people of Treegrass are not allowed guns. Why would we need guns if the government would always protect us?

Only police officers are allowed to carry guns, but they have spent years training in the town of Officials to learn how to use them properly. The police have never had to use their weapons in Treegrass before. As far as I'm aware, we are a pretty low-crime town. I think the most severe crime someone has ever committed here was theft.

Before tonight, I had never heard the sound of a gun being fired. Of course, I have seen and heard a gunshot before in old videos of the war with the Fritts, but that was different. The real thing is much louder, and it echoes. The videos always made it seem like the shots were quieter and somehow not as dangerous and scary.

The reality of the situation is sinking in, and I can't help but feel a sense of dread and loneliness. We were so unprepared. So innocent. I am standing in an empty room holding a weapon that I never imagined I would ever be in my grasp.

I tuck the gun in the waistband of my jeans and hope I will not ever have to use it. I bring it with me as protection. I take the small flashlight with me as well because why not?

The only protection I have apart from the gun is myself. I don't think it would be in my best interest to try and fight a guard since I have never fought anyone other than Devin before. Fighting Devin can't even be considered a real fight, it was only ever play fighting, it was nothing serious. Given the gravity of the situation, I don't want to take a chance and try fighting someone today, especially not a guard.

I go through the rest of the bags, but they all seem to be the same as the first few I looked through. There were no more guns or any other weapons, so I move away from the table to leave.

I press my ear up to the door to try and listen for any guards that may be walking around on the other side. I don't hear anyone talking or walking, and there are no gunshots, so I crack the door open and look outside. Nobody's around.

I step outside, and once again, I am in direct lighting. I move to where Aiden and I were hiding before behind the booth and assess my situation. The guard is still standing at the entrance of the show tent, his attention focused on something in the distance.

The building I was just in is closer to where this spot is. To get to the other building, I would have to cross an open area in the light, but the guard in front of the tent would surely see me. I have to find a way to get to the other building without getting caught. I could do this by looking for dark places to hide, or I could just wing it and run across the open area through the lights to get to the room. It may be dumb, but I chose the second option.

Moving through the shadows would take too long, and there aren't many dark places over here to begin with, so it would be a challenge anyway. I would like a third and easier option, but it does not look like there is one. I need to get to that second building. By now, Aiden is probably making his way to the kitchen, and the other guards will be coming back my way at any minute. I don't have the luxury of taking my time.

I inch my way up to the edge of the booth and contemplate my chances of making it to the second building if I were to try and run there. All the lights are on over here, and there are also lights all around building two. There is no way that the guard in front of the show tent won't see me. The door is facing in my direction, similar to the first building, so the guard in front of the show tent will only see me for a few seconds before I disappear from his view, thanks to the building.

The main question now is, do I run to building number two, or do I try walking there casually and hope the guard thinks I am one of them?

I freeze for a second as a thought occurs to me.

There were guard jackets on the back of the door of building one. Maybe if I put one on, then I will blend in better, and I can make it to building two without getting shot.

I make my way back over to building one as fast as I can and go back inside. Once the door is closed, I look at the coat hanger on the back. There are a few dark gray guard vests and jackets on it, and I steal the one that looks the smallest, which is not that small.

I put the jacket on and I immediately know that it's too large for me. The sleeves go a few inches past my hands, and if I were to zip the jacket up, it would look like I am wearing a dress. I roll the sleeves up to my wrists, and then I press my ear to the door.

I am already a gun and flashlight thief, so I might as well be a jacket thief, too. Hopefully, I will blend in more with the darkness, and the guards will think that I am one of them and leave me alone.

If this does not work, then the guard will most likely shoot me or chase me down. There is probably about a fifty-fifty chance that either of these options will happen.

I want a second to think before returning outside, but I have already taken up too much time.

I take the chance and open the door again, leaving the first building. I keep my head up and look straight ahead, walking as though I have places to be, which is technically true. I hold my breath as I make it halfway to the building.

I tell myself that the guard at the front of the show tent will think I am just like another guard—a guard with a very oversized jacket on.

Each step I take feels like an eternity. The seconds seem to pass slower, and I feel as though I am walking in a dream, fighting to move my body just one step more.

Once I get to the door of building two, I let out the breath I was holding. My knees are trembling, and I can't seem to keep my hands from shaking with fear.

I lean up against the door and close my eyes. I listen to hear if any footsteps are coming my way, and when I don't hear any, I take a few deep breaths to calm myself down. If that guard came over here and looked at me close up, he would definitely know that I am not a guard.

When I don't hear anything else besides the leaves on the trees near me moving with the wind, I take that as a good sign and go inside.

Chapter 17

Like the previous building, this one is brightly lit up on the inside. Other than that, the two buildings are entirely different.

The first building was a near empty canvas, but this one is a chaotic rats nest cluttered with papers all over the tables and walls. Papers carpet the six rectangular tables that line the four walls. Each table is so covered to the point that I can't tell what color they are.

On the back wall, there is a map of the whole town of Treegrass, with the carnival drawn onto the town. This has to be the room with the information Vesper told Aiden about.

As I step further into the room, I can't help but berate myself for my lack of caution since I did not consider the possibility of a guard being in here ready to shoot me. I make a mental note to change that, and then I turn my attention to the thousands of papers scattered across the nearest table.

Aiden's instructions echo in my mind. He said to look for anything about where they might be taking the carnival to next and to find a map. The school had shown us a map of the New World before, but it was too vast and complex to commit to memory. If I could steal a map for the Jumpers, then that would surely help them go to another town and warn them of what is coming.

The first table of papers is full of drawings of the games we played here. There are drawings of the rock wall, the triangles, the shark game, and more. Devin and I must have missed some of the games because there are a few drawings here that I do not recognize.

I flip through the papers to see if there is anything that could be useful on this table, and when I see nothing, I move on to the next.

The second table has papers with many people's names on them—just one list after another. I don't know who these people are or if they are important, so I take the notepad that Aiden gave me out of my back pocket and write down some of the names.

Izzy Soto

Leo Tyler

Georgina Donati

Issac Rowland

Karl Blackwood

Since I don't want to waste too much time, I stop writing down names and start looking through the papers again.

I shuffle through more and more papers and start getting frustrated by the New World's inability to be organized. How did they manage to kill us if they can't even get their documents in order? It's like being hunted by a raccoon, and somehow, the raccoon is winning.

After what seems like forever, I finally find a list of the names of the eighteen towns in the New World. Except this list only has seventeen town names. Of course, they would not include themselves. I quickly pull out Aiden's notepad again and write down the names in the order they appear on the list. I don't know if this is the exact order in which the deadly carnival will go, but I keep it in order just in case.

I put the paper down and look through the rest of the papers laying around. I come across a paper with Governor Davies' name written on it, titled Saving Life. I have no idea what that is supposed to mean because, from my perspective, it looks like he wants to take life since he is killing most of us. Who is he saving other than himself and the others in the town of Officials?

No one is safe, and no one is being saved. I guess that is not true. Aiden and the Jumpers saved us, but no one saved them or the town of Redseed.

I skim over some of what the paper says, and I immediately put it down when I see the words The removal of a portion of our country's population has become the only solution we have found to work without fail. I want to burn this stupid lie, but I think that would give away the fact I am in here.

I move on to look through the rest of the papers, and I manage to find a map. It is just as I remember, very confusing. The map is confusing because so many towns are separated by the large green and yellow spaces between them. This area is called no man's land. We were told no man's land was too dangerous and that a person could only go out there if they had a valid reason and were accompanied by the military or guards. My fingers trace over the intricate lines on the map as I wonder about how much the New World has lied to us.

There is a pretty big rolled up map that I decide to leave behind, its size and complexity making it too impractical to bring with me. However, a slightly smaller one catches my eye, and I decide to fold it up and put it in my pocket. There is no way that I am going to waste any more time in here by trying to draw an exact replica of the map and put it into the notepad.

I shuffle through the papers once again to see if I missed anything, but I don't think I have. I step back from the tables and look around the room again. The four walls are almost bare, and the room is windowless, so there is nothing I could miss there. The tables are cluttered with papers that mean mostly nothing to me. As I back up further closer to the door, I catch the sight of a small drawer on the far table that I don't remember checking.

I move over to it and quickly open it. There is nothing inside but a small laptop. I wish I could say I was surprised, but I'm not. Laptops are so expensive that only government officials and police officers can afford them. Some teachers in our school all joined together to buy one a few years ago, and I thought I would never hear them stop talking about it.

They would go on and on about what it could do. It could show multiple readings or files all at once, and it could even analyze those files and show you the similarities and differences between them. The laptop could download all your information and send that information straight to the police if anything were to happen to you. If you laid it flat on the table and clicked on a particular option, then it could show you a 3D version of whatever you were looking at. That was everyone's favorite option.

But most importantly, the laptop has some of the best security features. If you wanted to put a password on it, you could. I don't mean any regular stupid password that you would use to make your friend or sibling guess if he wanted to get into your fort as a kid.

No, I mean a password that a person could put a whole series of hidden buttons that someone has to hit in a particular order to unlock the laptop. If you didn't want a regular password like that, then you could choose to have a face recognition password or one with a voice activation option to unlock it.

There is an option for the laptop owner that if the wrong person tries to get in or fails to guess the password, the computer could take a picture of you so that the laptop owner would know who was trying to break in. This is a good security measure, but the teachers in my school never chose it since they felt sure enough that no one would try to get in.

I take the laptop out of the drawer and place it on the table. If I open the laptop and it's locked, then I know I have checked everything in this room, and I'll go. If there is no password or it has been unlocked, then maybe I could find something better than a few names and a map.

I know that the camera for facial recognition will be in the top center of the screen, so I slowly open it so I can put my hand over the camera. I don't know what would happen if the wrong person tries to unlock the laptop. Will it take my picture and send it to the police or the town of Officials? Or maybe since the government likes killing people as of lately, perhaps it will fire out a bullet right into my brain. That last one might be a little extreme, but I am not taking any chances, given the circumstances.

When the laptop is mostly opened, the screen lights up, and I am met with an image of the three heads of government staring right at me. Their heads are so prominent on the screen that I am taken by surprise, and I almost take my hand off the camera. I hold my hand onto the camera a little tighter and look around at the screen.

Besides the three faces of what I am now going to refer to as our nation's three biggest idiotic assholes, there is nothing else on the screen. There must be a hidden button or passcode, or it needs me to take my hand off the camera so it can use its facial recognition. I am about to close the laptop when a notification pops up.

You have thirty seconds to unlock.

A timer is shown counting down from thirty, and I start to panic. What happens after thirty seconds? Does it just turn off, does it shoot me, or does the whole thing just blow up?

I seriously hate the government. Just like their vague explanation for what happens to the red light people, their laptops are also ambiguous.

I don't bother sticking around to find out what happens if I fail to unlock the laptop, so I close it and put it back in the empty drawer. Once I close the drawer, I turn around and head for the door. If there is nothing else useful in this room, then there is no reason for me to waste any more time here. I need to get to the kitchen to meet back up with Aiden.

I reach for the handle, but the door starts opening before I touch it. A wave of terror hits me, and I take multiple steps backward until my back hits the end of a paper-filled table. A guard walks in and freezes when he sees me, just as I do when I see him.

The male guard is on the younger side. His blond hair is slicked back, and his uniform is perfect—no wrinkles or stains. His eyes skim me over, and I know that he can tell I am not another guard and that I shouldn't be in here. I catch the sight of his gun strapped onto his waist, and I am reminded of my own gun.

When the guard takes a step toward me, I quickly pull out the gun from my waistband and point it at him before he can reach his own weapon.

"Hands up and close the door," I say, trying to sound like the most confident person in the world.

The guard looks at me for another second, then does what I said. "How did you get in here?" He asks and tries, taking a step closer to me.

I hold the gun up to point at his head, "I don't recommend stepping any further," I hope my voice comes out as serious as I mean. "I don't want to shoot you, but I will if I have to."

The guard nods in understanding, and then I continue, "Is anyone else expected to come through that door?"

The guard looks at the door and then back to me, "Not that I know of."

"How many guards are out there?"

"I don't know."

"Don't lie, I want an answer."

"I don't know." He says again a little louder.

I decided to let the question go since he would probably lie about it anyway. Besides, it doesn't really matter how many guards are outside that door. If there are more than one, then I am as good as dead.

A new question hits me. "How many innocent lives have you taken today? How many people have you killed?"

He closes his eyes for a second before answering, "Why would that answer matter? You aren't going to believe me anyway."

He is right, but it does not change the anger I have because of him and his fellow shooters.

"Move," I tell him, motioning with my gun to the other side of the room. He nods, then slowly takes one step to the side, then another, and another. Once he is standing on one side of the room and I am on the opposite side, which is closest to the door, I decide to make my move.

Without saying another word, I quickly open the door and sprint out of the room as fast as possible. I don't turn back to see if the guard is behind me or if other guards are chasing after me. I just run as fast as I can in the direction that I think Aiden and I came from.

Chapter 18

I am running so fast that I am not even sure my feet are touching the ground anymore. I just keep pushing my feet to keep moving as fast as they can.

I can't let them catch me.

I don't even know how many of them are behind me. For all I know, there could be one or ten, or maybe I have finally caught a break, and there is no one behind me.

I don't take the chance of looking back, I just keep moving my feet as fast as I can away from the building. I need to find where the Ferris wheel is. The room is over there somewhere, but I can't take a minute to look around since there are potentially dangerous people chasing after me.

I decide to take a few random turns, and I end up not having the slightest clue as to where I am. I decide to take a sharp turn to the left, but I end up running straight into one of the guards. I stumble backwards, almost falling to the ground. The guard grabs my arm, and fear rushes through my body.

All I can think about is Aiden returning to the group and telling Devin that I am gone, probably dead. I do the only thing I can think of and try to punch at the guard with my other arm and kick at him. He is strong, but when I punch down with my free arm at his arm that is holding mine, his grip loosens, and I am able to free myself and start running again.

I am practically stumbling away from the guard, but once I see that the guards have caught up to me, I quickly correct myself. I have to doge multiple arms reaching for me as I run to the right and down a row of games, but none of them touch me. I do my best to lose them, and I think it is working. When I look behind me, they are about fifteen feet away.

I make another turn, and when I do, I catch the sight of a booth that no longer has its lights on. I run and hide behind it. I sit down on the ground and wait to hear the sounds of the guards running by.

I stay in place and try to catch my breath. Breathe in, breathe out, breathe in and out. After about thirty seconds, I hear the sound of boots hitting the ground, and I crawl further into my hiding spot. The sound gets louder, and I know they are coming my way. It is not until right now that I realize that I have not heard a single gunshot being fired at me. The guard who grabbed me didn't even pull out his gun or threaten to shoot me.

It would be wise to shoot at me while I was running from them, so why didn't they? From what I can hear, there are multiple guards heading my way, so they had a pretty good opportunity to kill me. I got out. I disobeyed them by escaping. Shouldn't they want to kill me? I guess I should be thankful that they didn't, but I can't help but wonder why.

The footsteps get closer and closer until they are right by the booth I am in, then they run past it. I let out a breath of relief. Another minute goes by before I hear more boots coming my way. Really? How many people did they send out for me? I know I am practically a fugitive, but do they really need so many people to find one person?

I don't move as they run by, but I do notice that one of them has stopped somewhere by me.

A static voice is heard, "Branson, what's your status on the girl?"

The voice of the guy standing by my booth responds, "We haven't found her yet, sir, but we will. I have guys searching every booth and tent as we speak. We'll find her."

There is more static heard, and the guy walks off. The police in our town frequently use walkie-talkies to talk to one another, and from the sound of things, the guards here are also using them.

In my second-to-last year of schooling, one guy in my grade was dared to steal a walkie-talkie from one of the policemen. The guy was known not to make the smartest decisions, so he tried the dare. He was caught instantly. While it was dumb, it was also funny to watch him run up to a police car, stick his hand through the window, pull out the walkie-talkie, and then turn around to come face to face with one of the police officers.

If what I heard from the guards using the walkie-talkies is true, then they will find me soon. I need to move.

I peek my head out of the side of the booth and look around. I don't see or hear anyone, so I slowly stand up and move towards the direction in which I came. I don't think that the guards would immediately start checking the direction in which I came from. They would first check the direction I ran in, right?

I move a few feet away and hide behind another game with its lights off. I continue this process of moving booth to booth and sometimes booth to tree, until I come across the main tent again.

The four guards are back standing at the entrance of the main tent, and once again, there are quite a few guards walking around the area. The door to the small building that the guard caught me in is wide open. The same three guards keep going in and out of the room, talking to one another.

Their body language and facial expressions tell me that they are under a lot of stress. I am glad they are stressed. I am stressed. They are the ones who came in here and told us they were going to kill half our town. They are the ones who opened fire on us for trying to escape the show tent. I do not pity them.

I can't hear what they are saying, but I can guess it has something to do with me. They are most likely trying to figure out what I was doing in there and if I took anything.

It was only a map... from that room. The gun was from the first room, and from what I can see, no one is investigating that building.

I know I can't stay here forever, so I try to find the Ferris wheel again. I am pretty sure it should be located somewhere in front of the main tent, so I move in that direction, once again going from booth to booth.

There are a few times when I have to stop and duck down further in the booth so that I am not spotted. The guards are still looking for me, and it seems like they have started walking in what sounds like groups of two or three.

I don't get it. Don't they have better things to do than look for me?

I wait until they pass before moving along. When I get further from the tent, I notice that there is less light because there are fewer games on. I use this to my advantage since it is easier for me to move undetected in the dark.

The area I am in now is almost entirely dark, and for some reason, it feels more safe than it should be. Dark places are supposed to creep people out, but given the situation, I feel just fine. I take a turn in the direction that I think the giant wheel would be in, but I can't seem to find it.

The Ferris wheel is huge and lit up, or at least it was earlier. How can I keep missing it?

I get comfortable moving in the dark, and I start walking while trying to look up above some of the tents and booths to see if I can spot the Ferris, but I can't. I guess I get too comfortable walking like this since I almost walk right in front of two guards.

If it weren't for the guards talking to each other, then I would have been spotted in all my stupid glory for sure. I quickly move to hide behind the wall of some building, and I shrink back further until I hit a tree. The voices are coming closer, and without a second thought, I start climbing the tree.

My body moves without me having to think much about it. Living in Treegrass, I think everyone here seems to have a natural-born talent for climbing trees. My body moves instinctively. I find myself ascending higher into the tree until I am at the same height as the top of the building.

I am not really sure if I should climb onto the roof or stay in the tree. I think the guards would be more likely to cheek the tree than the roof of a building, so I lean one leg over to the roof and then my other leg. Once I am standing on the flat roof, I duck down and make my way over to the edge where the guards are walking by. I want to make sure they are far enough away and no more guards are coming, before I get down and find my way to the kitchen.

The two guards are still talking to one another as they walk by the building. Unfortunately, to my dismay, they are walking slowly. My frustration grows. Don't they know I've got some place to be right now? What if I am taking too long, and Aiden thinks I have been captured or killed? Aren't they supposed to be in a hurry to find me?

"I can't believe we are staying up this late. When do you think we'll be done here and can go home?" One guard asks the other guard.

"I don't know, probably when we catch the girl."

This piques my curiosity, and I strain to hear more.

The guards continue talking, "Danny must be such an idiot to let that girl get away. He went to the academy, he got the training, so how did he let her get away? Shouldn't he have easily been able to tackle her down and restrain her?"

"Yeah well, he's young and has only just graduated from the academy a few months ago. You know how it is. Anyway, from what I heard, he tried chasing the girl down, but she was too fast. You can't blame the boy for that."

"You can blame the boy for that, and I will. I want to get some sleep, but this girl on the loose is preventing that. They should have never let the others go back to camp early. If the others stayed, then they would have never gotten out of the tent in the first place." There is another sound, but I can't identify the source, "She is also preventing me from getting out of this stupid bug-infested hell hole."

"Listen buddy, we all want some sleep, but complaining about it isn't going to make us catch her any sooner. We need to find out where her friends are hiding."

Where my friends are hiding? Do they mean Aiden? My brother? The Jumpers?

"We're not going to mess up again like in Tundris. That made us look bad, and the Governors won't like to hear about it happening again here. We are not going to let anyone escape. It's only been a few hours. They are probably hiding somewhere in here, and we just are too stupid to know where. He said the girl was on the younger side, so she is probably hiding in some small place. Once we find her, everything will be okay."

"Why don't you think they're out there in the town or beyond the borders?"

"Because the guys at the front gate said that they have seen no one leave the carnival, and let's be real, no one wants to go outside the town borders into no man's land."

I want to ask what they know about no man's land, but given my situation, I don't think they would answer me and then let me go.

"We will find the girl, and she will lead us to the other thirty-six people missing from the count, and maybe, if we're lucky, we will also find out about the other people who are missing from the first town. We would be idiots to think they didn't have something to do with this."

Chapter 19

Their voices start getting too quiet for me to hear, but I think I have listened to enough.

The guards want to catch me so they can find out where all the people who escaped went. They don't think we hid in no man's land, but they do believe the Jumpers had something to do with us getting out of the tent. That means they do not know much.

They don't know all the facts, but they do have an idea about the Jumpers' involvement here. They know the Jumpers are here but do not know to what extent or where they are. The less they know, the better. If they end up capturing me, they should just kill me because I will not be giving up any information. I will not put Devin's life in harm's way.

They think we are hiding somewhere in the carnival, but they don't know that the Jumpers got us out and into the trees where we will be leaving in the morning or, should I say, where they will be leaving in the morning. If Aiden and I are not back before sunrise, then they will leave without us.

And what about no man's land? I know that the government thinks it's dangerous, but how dangerous can it really be? The government mentioned a long time ago that there are wild animals out there, along with potential human threats, but they never really specified any further. The details about no man's land remain uncertain.

Are these dangers of no man's land real, or did they lie about that too? How do I know if anything they have ever said has been true or not?

I no longer believe a word they have ever said, but at the same time, I am torn between my disbelief and my fear of the unknown. I don't want to go into no man's land and learn how dangerous it is by getting attacked by someone or something. What if what I discover out there beyond my town borders is worse than what is currently inside?

But then again, the Jumpers said they have a camp a few miles from here, and they didn't mention anything about the dangers of no man's land. I didn't think to ask. Maybe they are withholding important information about its dangers, and I just don't know it. Once again, I am reminded of the fact that I don't know the Jumpers, and I should not blindly trust them either.

When I am convinced that the guards are far enough away that they won't see me, I look over the edge of the building to see where I am. It is dark, but I can make out the outline of a few booths. I look straight ahead into the darkness and try to find the Ferris wheel.

I feel like a crazy person constantly looking for something that is not there. The Ferris wheel was real, right? I did not just imagine its existence. It was a big circular thing lit up in the sky, it has to be here somewhere.

I keep looking, and I manage to catch the sight of something slightly to the right of where I am. A small reflection of light reflects off of one of the buckets of the Ferris wheel.

I am filled with relief now that I can find my way to the kitchen from here. Hopefully, Aiden will still be there waiting for me. I feel like I have taken so many detours, and now I am taking too long. Aiden probably thinks I have been captured or killed and has moved on without me.

Since the Ferris wheel is to the right, that means I must have passed it while getting here. In my defense, I was looking for a colorful, lit-up Ferris wheel, not a dark piece of metal in the night sky. I look down to see what building I am on top of. I know that I am not on top of the kitchen since the Ferris wheel was to the left of that.

As I look, I see a big letter M, which looks like a W from my angle. I don't bother to read the rest of the letters. Of course, I would be right at the Mirror Maze. If only Aiden and I had planned on meeting back here instead of in the kitchen, then we would both be walking out of here right now.

I make my way back to the tree and climb down it. At least I know where I am now, and I know exactly how to get to the kitchen. The way back to the kitchen is pretty straightforward, so I start moving in the direction where the games were.

I think it would have been a better idea if the guards had turned all the lights in the carnival on instead of off, but I am not going to argue with their logic. The darkness is helping me right now. I say turn all the lights off so I can get to the kitchen easier.

If all the lights were on right now, I would be sweating at the thought of getting caught in the light for all the guards to see. But on the other hand it would make it easier for me to see the guards as well. I wouldn't have to question whether or not if every sound I hear is from a guard or something else.

I make my way behind the row of game booths and start quietly walking from one booth to another. It is quiet as I make my way behind the first few booths. It's not as dark as it was over by the Mirror Maze, but it's also not as bright as it was earlier when Aiden and I were walking over here.

As I make my way closer to the Ferris wheel, I notice that the open area we crossed before is slightly brighter, and more guards are walking by. The first two times I hear footsteps, I crouch down behind the booth and cram myself as far as I can into the little spots of darkness. Since nothing happened and there were no guards even remotely stepping towards where I was hiding, I stopped forcing myself to fit in the shadows and instead just stood behind the booth.

That is where I am now, standing like a creeper behind a booth, waiting to hear the sound of boots walking off in the distance.

It takes about fifteen seconds for a guard to walk by me, and I wait another thirty seconds and move to another booth to ensure the guard is far enough away so that he won't see me. It's a tedious process but a safe one. The guards walk by my area every three minutes or so. They could all be different guards or the same guard. I don't really know, nor do I care.

Making it to the kitchen is all that matters right now.

I keep moving from booth to booth until I come to the exact spot where we crossed over from the kitchen. I watch as the guards frequently walk by. It's like when one guard finally leaves, another one enters. Getting to the other side is going to be tricky.

I stand in the shadows, waiting for any opening that I can get. I think about causing a distraction, but I fear that it would only draw more guards around to this side of the carnival, and that would increase the chances of the guards finding the kitchen. That's assuming that they haven't already.

I notice that I am never going to get the perfect opportunity to run to the other side, so I decide to do something a little risky.

When one guard is walking by, and his back is facing towards me and where I am going, I make a run for the booth in the middle of the opening. When I get there, I sit down in the corner of the booth and wait to hear the next guard go by. After the next guard walks by and has his back towards me, I run the rest of the way to the alley that leads to the kitchen.

When I reach the other side, I put my back against the wall and wait to hear if anyone saw me. When no noise is heard, I start walking down the alleyway and eventually come to the kitchen door.

I am hesitant to go inside since there is a chance that Aiden won't be in there. I think about the fact that he could have gotten caught, but then my brain reminds me that if the guards caught Aiden, then they would not be searching so hard for me. I then think about if he left me here, maybe I took too long, and he assumed that I was taken or killed.

I push all of those bad possibilities out of my head and tell myself that Aiden is in the room. All I have to do is open the door, and I will see him standing there waiting for me. We will quickly catch up with each other about what I found in the room and about the guards looking for us and then Aiden will lead the two of us out of here safely just like before.

I open the kitchen door and am immediately reminded of how dark the room is. I walk in and close the door behind me.

"Aiden," I whisper.

There is no response, so I try again, "Aiden, are you in here?"

I step further into the kitchen, but when I hear nothing, I lose all the possible hope I have left, and I turn around to leave.

Before I can take one step to the door, a hand is thrown over my mouth, and I am practically dragged down to the floor. Every ounce of my body is put on high alert and I start thinking about how on earth I could fight this person and make a break for the door.

I start kicking my legs at the person and throwing my arms around as hard as I can, but I stop when I hear Aiden's voice in my ear, "Stop. Sam, Stop. We are not alone in here," he says very quietly.

Chapter 20

I try not to freak out at this information, but when someone tells you that you are not alone in here, it is hard not to. The room is pitch black, and the only sound I hear is Aiden's breathing behind me.

Who else is in this room? Is it just one person, or are there more? How long has Aiden been in this room with another person or people?

I hear some shuffling on the other side of the room, and I just hope that it is another person like us and not some guard. Aiden moves his body so that he is now sitting in front of me, and I am between him and the wall. He begins to move away from me, and I grab his arm to pull him back.

"Where are you going?" I whisper to him.

Aiden whispers back to me, "I think he is like us, running from the guards. I'll be right back." Then he moves away from me, and I let him.

If the other person in here is just like us, then he is not a threat, and we could bring him back with us and get him to safety. If this other person is like us, then maybe others who escaped from the show tent are still around in the carnival. Maybe my Dad is still out there after all. Perhaps he is the one in the room with us.

I try not to get my hopes up with that last thought.

After Aiden walks away, it is quiet for a few seconds until I hear the sound of some feet shuffling around. About two seconds later, the sound of movement gets louder until an even louder thunk is heard. My eyes widen in fear, and I immediately get up from where I am sitting and try to find my way around the room to Aiden.

I make my way around a corner of what I assume is a table, and since my eyes are still adjusting to the dark, all I find is a big blob of darkness on the ground. The blob moves around, and I know that it must be Aiden and the other guy wrestling on the floor. Who has the upper hand right now? I don't know, but I have to make sure they stop fighting. It is getting too loud, and a guard will probably hear it if they are close enough to the kitchen.

"There are guards patrolling this area, so please stop," I whisper shout at them. "Or at least fight quieter, please."

The big blob on the ground shuffles around some more until it comes to a complete stop.

Suddenly, the voice of an adult man is heard, "I can't let them get me. They'll kill me. You don't understand. You have to let me go. I was here-" His words get cut off by what I am assuming is Aiden's hand.

The guy starts trying to wiggle away from Aiden, but Aiden holds him back.

"Listen, dude, if you don't stop moving and talking, then they are going to kill all of us," Aiden says to the guy. This seems to get the guy's attention since he stops struggling in Aidens arms and he gets quiet for a minute.

"Okay, I am going to take my hand away from your mouth, and then I am going to let you go. When I do, you are not going to scream or talk too loud. Got it?" Aiden says while sounding a little out of breath.

My eyes adjust more, and I can see the guy nod his head. Aiden moves away from the guy, stands up, and walks over to me. The guy stays sitting on the ground and doesn't say anything.

The room is quiet again, so I decide to break the silence with the most lame question I can think of, "So... what's your name?"

It is still hard to make anything out in the dark, but I swear that I see the guy look away from me with annoyance and then back to me before saying, "Ethen," with some anger in his voice.

I don't understand. Doesn't this dude know that we are not with the guards and we are not trying to kill him? If anything, we are trying to help him. Why does he have to have an attitude?

"I'm Aiden, and this is," Aiden pauses and looks at me. "You know what, I don't think you told me your name."

I think about that for a second, and I guess he is right. I haven't given him my name.

"Sam," I tell Aiden, and then I remember the other guy in the room. "I'm Sam," I say awkwardly, this time facing Ethen.

"Great, now that we got that out of the way, what are the two of you doing here? This is my hiding spot," Ethen says. "I found it, and I plan on using it for as long as possible. The two of you being here is compromising my safe space."

"This isn't a safe space," I tell him. "There are guards all around here patrolling. They are searching everywhere for anyone who escaped. They have been checking the game booths and it is only a matter of time before they look in here as well. You are not safe. None of us are."

"Also," Aiden says, "let it be known that first of all, I was here first, so that makes it my spot. Second, we are not your enemy. We did nothing wrong, so lose the attitude. Third, Sam and I are planning on getting the hell out of here. If you want to, you can come with us, but you're going to have to leave the negativity in this room."

The guy opens his mouth to say something but then looks behind us and quickly shuts it. I turn to look to see what caught Ethen's attention at the same time as Aiden does. When I look behind me at the room, I see the outline of a person through the door window. I know that Aiden saw it too, because when I look back at him, I see his expression is the same as mine. We quickly get down and hide behind the table closer to Ethen.

I hear the door open, and my heart starts racing. The table isn't the standard four-legged table, it is more like a countertop, so if the guard were to spot us, then he would have to come around to our side of the table where we are hiding. I catch the sight of a faint light on the other side of the room from the guard's flashlight, and I know it is only a matter of time before he finds us. I put my hand on the waist of my pants where the gun is.

"What are you doing?" My heart nearly jumps out of my chest when the guard says this. Does he know we are here? Does he think we are other guards? Is there a way where we can talk our way out of this?

Ethen looks like a panicked little kid who did something wrong and is about to get yelled at by his mother. I just hope he doesn't scream, cry, or pee his pants. Now that I can see him a little better, it looks like Ethen may look to be in his forties, but he definitely doesn't act like it. I think I hear a whimper come out of his mouth when the sound of a footstep comes our way.

You have got to be kidding me. How has this guy lived this long? Aiden shoots Ethen a look, and Ethen shrinks down further to the ground quietly. He squeezes his eyes shut, and I shoot Aiden a questioning glance. Aiden's face says 'You have got to be kidding me,' and I can tell that the both of us are going to have our hands full when it comes to Ethen.

Then, a voice closer to us responds, "I thought I heard something, man." The light moves around the room, but the guard doesn't come our way. "It was probably just a mouse or something. Let's go."

The door closes, but none of us move. We sit in the silent darkness and wait to ensure the guards are far enough away to start talking again.

When I think they are far enough away, I whisper to Aiden, "I wasn't exaggerating before. There are guards everywhere out there, more than before. We need to be quiet."

Aiden looks in the direction of the door and then back at me, "What happened out there? Are you okay?" He starts looking at me, trying to check for injuries, but I assure him I'm fine.

"I'm okay. There wasn't anything in the first room, so I went to the second one. I just ran into some trouble in the second room, but I am fine." I try to make it sound like nothing although it scared the crap out of me. "I got the names of the towns and a map." I take the notepad and map out of my pocket and hand them to him. "There was a long list of names on multiple pieces of paper. I don't know how useful they will be, so I only wrote a few down."

"That's alright, you did good. The map will be very helpful in figuring out where to go next," Aiden says.

"A guard walked into the room when I was about to leave. I got away, but it caused more guards to go and look for me. For us." I look at Aiden in the eyes to make sure he is listening. "They know people are missing. I heard the guards talking about it. They have been doing a headcount and found thirty-six people missing from Treegrass, and they know that people escaped from your town, too. They have their suspicions about your involvement here."

Aiden processes this information, "Do they know where they have gone or how they got out? Do they know it's the Jumpers?"

"I don't know, that was all I heard," I tell Aiden.

He looks troubled by this but doesn't say anything else.

"What are you two whispering about?" Ethen asks.

Aiden and I both look at him and then back to each other.

"What?" Ethen says, "I want to know. I think I have a right to know, right? If I am going to be joining the two of you in getting out of here, then I should be filled in on what is going on." Ethen states this as if it were a fact. The annoying part is, he is not wrong.

Chapter 21

Ethen has a right to know what we are talking about, but I just feel like he should not be fully trusted with this information yet. He is not exactly the nicest guy, and for all I know, we could give him some information, and then he could spill this information to the guards if they ever were to capture him.

While I do not anticipate Ethen falling into the hands of the guards, the possibility remains. Now that there is an increased guard presence due to them all finding me and chasing me down, getting to the Mirror Maze will be hard. Ethen is going to make it even more challenging if he keeps acting the way he has.

He is scared. That is understandable. What is not understandable is that he acts pissed off toward us. He keeps his body turned partly away from us, and I notice that he only maintains eye contact with Aiden, not me. I assume he maybe does not like women, but it doesn't look like he likes Aiden anymore than me. He keeps looking at Aiden as if he is about to charge at him at any moment. This behavior tells me that he is not very fond of us, and he would give up information about us if it meant saving himself.

I know that Aiden wouldn't tell the guards anything if he were captured because he has risked his life to get himself and the people from his town out of Tundris, and he helped our people get out of this place. I wouldn't say anything to the guards because then I would be putting Devin's life at risk. They would have to kill me before I told them anything that could put my brother in danger.

Aiden thinks before speaking, "Two months ago, the government set up a carnival just like this one in my town, Tundris. At the end of the night, they did the exact thing they are doing here. They started killing people. A group of us got out, and we have since been trying to get to other towns before the carnival gets to them. We call ourselves the Jumpers. We are not affiliated with the New World government or any other. We are just trying to survive. Once we get out of here, you can join us if you want."

The guy looks at the two of us with curiosity, then relaxes more and puts his hands in his lap. "I came here with my three brothers tonight. They are all married and have kids, but we still thought it would be fun to challenge each other and see who could do the best in the games." Ethen sits back, and his eyes look to the side as if he were watching the memory happen right in front of him. "The games were fun. I can't help but wonder what the answers to some of the questions were. I like to think I did well on them, but who the hell knows."

Ethen stops talking for a second, and his mood gets sour. "My older brother Nick has always been the best kid. My parents have always favored him. He could simply do no wrong. He always got away with everything. Do you know what it is like to be the least favorite child?"

"All my brothers," Ethen points to nowhere in particular, "are successful and have purposeful jobs. But not Ethen. No, Ethen has no wife or kids, and Ethen works at the library cleaning up after everyone's lazy dirty asses. It is as if it was my fault. It is so hard to move up in the world here. There are simply not enough good, respectable jobs. Somebody has to do the less desirable work, and that person just so happens to be me."

"I wanted to be a firefighter, but the academy said I was too impulsive and wasn't learning fast enough. I then tried to be a police officer, but I kept failing the entry exam." Ethens clenches his jaw as if two strong magnets were the thing keeping his mouth closed. "Nick passed. Nick got to become a police officer," He struggles to say. "Nick got the best job in the whole fucking world."

"All night, we kept playing every game we could find, and I kept hoping to find a game that I could beat him in." Ethen brings his hand to cover half his face as he continues, "I tried. I really tried, but It was like no matter what I did, I couldn't win. I couldn't even get out of last place. My other brothers would laugh at me, but it wasn't my fault. The games were hard. I think Nick was cheating. I don't know how, but he had to be. He was winning every game."

I think about what Ethen says about the games. Every game Devin and I played was fair. I don't think someone could have cheated on them. By the way Ethen is acting, he probably lost fair and square. He just doesn't know how to handle failure.

Ethen takes his hand away from his face, and I can see that his facial expression is full of anger and probably some hatred. "Back when we were in school together, Nick would always charm the other girls into giving him whatever he wanted. He probably did the same thing tonight, but I didn't notice. He was probably telling them to make me lose on purpose, so then they could have a laugh when I lost yet again. At the end of the night, when they told us about the boxes, the light on his box was green, of course, and mine was red."

He sighs in frustration, "I should have had the green light, and he should have gotten the red one. It was so not fair."

I am surprised at what I am hearing. Did this guy really wish his brother dead? Does he know that a red light on the box means death? Does he know what he is saying right now?

I look at Aiden with worry and concern. Should we really be bringing him with us if he is practically insane? Having him around other people and kids might not be the best idea.

For a moment, Aiden looks like he is thinking, and then he looks back at Ethen, "You do realize that the people with the red lights were the ones getting killed, right?"

Ethen nods his head. "I know it sounds crazy, but you do not know what it has been like to grow up with them. I don't agree with our Governors about killing people in order to fix things, but since they were doing it anyway, then I would have liked for them to get Nick, maybe even Trevor and Elijah as well."

Yeah, this dude definitely has a few screws loose in his head.

Ethen turns to Aiden, "When you said you could get me out of here, do you mean the carnival or Treegrass? Because I would really like to get out of both. I hate it here."

This dude is definitely crazy. I have never heard of there being a murder here in Treegrass, but if I had, this guy would most likely be the killer. There is no way we can bring him with us.

"Yeah, I can get you out of here," Aiden says, and I whip my head around to look at him like he is just as insane as Ethen. He glances over at me, but I can't tell what he is thinking. His face is expressionless.

I open my mouth to question Aiden's decision, but when I do, the door to the room opens, and we all immediately go still.

"What are you doing, man?" A voice asks.

"I thought I heard something in here earlier, and I want to make sure it is clear before we head back," another voice responds.

The sound of footsteps gets closer to our side of the table. Aiden moves so that both of his feet are flat on the ground, and it looks like he is crouching rather than sitting. The light from the guard's flashlight makes it clear that he is heading our way, and I once again put my hand on the gun. Within seconds, the light is on us, and before I can even process what to do, Aiden dives for the guard's legs, and the two of them end up on the ground fighting each other.

The guard in the doorway has one of his hands on his gun and is pointing it at Aiden and the guard on the ground. His other hand is on the walkie-talkie. He starts to press a button on it, and it looks like he is about to say something, so I quickly pull my gun out and point it at him. The guard immediately closes his mouth and starts pointing his gun between me and the two people fighting on the floor.

"Don't even think about it," I say, making sure that the guard hears how serious I am about shooting him. He was most likely one of the people who had a hand in killing a portion of my town tonight, so there is no reason I should spare his life. If he tries to shoot me or Aiden, then I will not hesitate to shoot him.

The guard gives me a hard, stern look that makes me think he does not take me seriously, so I take a step closer and give him my own stern look, which makes him waver a little bit.

"Drop the gun," I say, and the guard looks at me, debating, "Now!" I yell at him.

The guard lowers his handgun, and I glance over to the fight that is still happening on the floor. The guard at the door sees my temporary distraction and uses his hand that was previously on the walkie-talkie to push my arms to the side and knock the gun out of my hand.

I try to swing at him with my right arm, but I miss, and I am instead pushed to the ground. I can still hear Aiden and the other guard fighting only a few feet away, but I can't focus on them right now.

The guard that pushed me down goes to stand over me, and I manage to kick one of his kneecaps. The guard buckles slightly but does not entirely fall to the ground. If anything, all I made him do was get angry.

"Now you've done it kid," the guard says and goes to grab me on the ground. I try to push my arms out and kick my legs to push him away, but this doesn't work. In one quick motion, the guard lifts up his arm, and the next thing I know is that the world goes black.

Chapter 22

I'm running.

The bright lights of the carnival blur together as I run through the empty place I once found so beautiful.

I keep running.

I see people lying on the ground everywhere, but I just keep moving right by them.

I see the gate my family and I walked through just a few hours ago, and the doors are wide open.

On the other side of the gate, the sun rises above the horizon, creating beautiful designs in the sky. The orange, yellow, and hint of pink make me wish the earth could look like this all day.

I run through the open gate, leaving the carnival behind me.

I let my feet take me to where I'm going. There is no thought behind my movements. I just run, run, and run some more.

I don't run out of breath—I am not even sure I am still breathing—and I can't feel my feet hitting the ground below me. I can't feel anything.

I run, and I can't stop running.

All I can do is watch as I move past the houses I see every day. I run past the old mill where we used to take field trips as kids. I run past the flower store where my mother works. And then I run past the trees that Devin and I grew up climbing.

Before I know it, my feet are no longer running on solid, hard ground but a softer and bumper, familiar surface. I find myself running down a road I know very well, and I have a feeling that I know where my feet are taking me.

Is she there?

Is she alive?

Did they leave her unharmed?

Did she escape them?

I come to a halt right in front of my house. I look over at the empty chair on my front porch, and panic builds up inside of me. My mother was sitting in that chair just a few hours ago, but her and the blanket she was working on are no longer in sight. She could be inside, I think to myself.

I walk up to the front door, and I stare at the familiar carvings on the door for a second before opening the door slowly. I look around the living room, and when I don't see her, I start running into every room, yelling her name.

"Mom! Mom! Mom? Where are you? Mom! Mom! Are you here?"

I find myself running full speed again throughout the house, and when I am confident she is not here, I run out the back door.

My feet immediately stop in their tracks. There, lying on the ground in my backyard is my mother, next to her is my father, and next to him is my brother. Their eyes are open but lifelessly staring at me.

The air gets hard to breathe, and I feel tears filling up my eyes until I can no longer see properly.

"No... no... this isn't real... this isn't real."

I start yelling no more and more while I pinch my arm as hard as I can.

I hear my name being called in the distance, but I don't try to figure out where it's coming from.

"Sam!" The voice is louder now, and there is some sort of pressure on my shoulder.

I continue pinching myself while begging my body to wake up from this nightmare.

"Sam... Sam!"

I wake up with a jolt. "Sam!" Aiden is leaning over me with one hand on my shoulder and the other on the side of my face. The slight pain I feel on my upper cheek tells me that's where I got hit by the guard. I slowly sit up, and my head starts throbbing a little bit. I take a look around the room and see that it looks the same as before, aside from the two guards who are now lying on the floor in the corner.

As if reading my mind, Aiden says, "They're not dead, just unconscious. I tied their arms behind their backs and then to the table. I used a towel I found in one of the drawers to gag them so that if they wake up, they can't tell anyone anything until someone finds them and lets them go."

Aiden then looks at the side of my face, "He hit your head pretty hard. Are you okay?"

I give him a nod. "My head hurts a little, but I'll manage to survive."

"Good. If you were killed, then I don't think I would be able to go back out there. I would be getting hunted by shooters and your brother."

I smile a little at that statement.

"Cute. Now that the two of you have matching bruises, can we go now?"

I turn to glare at Ethen, I honestly forgot he was even here.

"We are going to go soon. I just wanted to make sure she was alright before we left." Aiden looks away from him with annoyance and then stands up. I stand too and look back at Aiden. He has a bruise along with a small cut on the side of his face, I assume from fighting the guard on the ground, and I wonder if he has any other injuries.

"Are you okay?" I ask him, knowing very well that he would probably lie to me if he wasn't since guys don't like to admit when they're in pain, or at least no guy I have ever met has.

"I'm fine. Just a few bruises."

Aiden gives me a small smile and then looks over to the two unconscious guards on the floor. He looks at them with a blank expression, but I know what he's probably thinking. He is probably torn between keeping them alive or killing them. Like me, he probably knows that the guards most likely had a hand in killing innocent people tonight. Or maybe he has seen them do it first-hand back in his town, I am not sure I want to know exactly what happened in his town. Unlike in Treegrass, no one was coming to warn Tundris or get them out.

I can't imagine what it must have been like for him, for all of them. Not knowing what to do, where to go, and who to trust. It must have been awful.

I'm glad he didn't kill them, but I'm still upset. These two guards were probably going to kill us or interrogate us to find out where the others went, so why should we spare them? I know why, but I'm not happy about it.

It's because we're human. We have morals, and while the shooters might not care about killing people, we do. We care, or at least I do. I assume Aiden does as well since they're not dead.

I think I would have shot the guard in the second room if he tried to shoot me, and I think I would have shot the guard who knocked me out in this room if he tried to kill me or Aiden. I just don't know what I would have done afterward if I had to do it. Killing them would make me become just like them, a killer.

Aiden looks at Ethen and then at me. "Okay, here is what we're going to do." Aiden goes over to the table where it looks like he has piled the guns. He hands Ethen and me one of the smaller guns. I get the same one I had before, the one that I took out of my waistband to use on the guard before he hit it out of my hands. "Keep these with you for your protection. Just in case." Aiden then grabs the bigger gun off the table and puts the strap around his shoulder. Aiden opens his mouth to say more, but Ethen cuts him off.

"Why do you get the big gun?" Ethen asks.

"Have you ever shot a gun before?" Aiden asks him back.

The question throws off Ethen, and he looks a little offended. "No. How hard can it be? What's the difference between starting with a big gun or a small one? They do the same thing, don't they? It's just that the bigger one does more damage."

The look Aiden gives him makes me think he is regretting ever meeting this guy and agreeing to get him out. Aiden sighs, looks down, and then back up at Ethen. "I get the big gun. You get the small one. Don't complain about it, and please stop talking."

I have to work hard to suppress my laughter. Aiden looks so done with this dude, and Ethen has no clue.

"No. I'm going to keep talking. I happen to like talking. I'll let the gun issue go, but I also want to know why we don't turn the flashlight on. Why are we discussing this in the dark when there is a perfectly fine flashlight right there?" Ethen asks. I honestly wonder if his mother dropped him on his head as a baby and then proceeded to continuously drop him on his head every day after.

Aiden takes the flashlight off the table and puts it in his pocket. "We're going to bring the flashlight with us, but we're not going to use it, no matter how dark it gets. Why? Because I said so, and also because the guards will see it. If they see the light, then they will see us, and I don't think you want that to happen now, do you?"

Ethen looks down like a little kid getting scolded, and he shakes his head in response. "I just want to get out of here."

"We're going to, but if we are going to get out of here alive, then we need to be smart about it." Aiden walks over to the door. "Now we are going to stick together, alright? Don't go wandering off or running away at the first sight of danger. We will be fine as long as we stay calm and rational. Now stay quiet, stay in the shadows, and follow us." Aiden says to Ethen.

Aiden opens the door and walks out into the all familiar pathway. This is now the second time I am walking down this path tonight. If you count going to the kitchen the first and second time, then it's the fourth time I have seen this place within the last few hours.

Aiden leads us down the path. I'm behind him, and Ethen is behind me. I take periodic glances behind me to make sure Ethen isn't going to panic and bolt, giving away our location. When we arrive at the end of the pathway, I watch Ethen's face as he realizes that we have to cross the open space that guards are frequently walking by.

Chapter 23

A iden walks us back a few feet on the path so we are further away from the light. "You were right about there being more guards," Aiden says to me. "We're going to have to take a different way around. It will probably take longer, but it will be safer."

I nod in agreement, and then I take another look at the now-sweating Ethen.

"You guys are insane," Ethen says. His voice is quiet enough for no one else to hear, but I do not miss the way panic and shrill make up his tone. "The guards are right over there, just a few feet away from us. If they are like that everywhere, then I am so dead. We should go back into the room and wait them out."

"There is no waiting them out," I say. "We got lucky with those two guards coming in the room. Pretty soon, there will be more coming to check the kitchen, and we might not get so lucky again. Besides, once those two guards wake up, they will be doing everything they can to alert the others. Going back there is not an option."

Aiden joins in, "Sam is right. We need to keep moving. If we go back into the room, we will be waiting with our backs into a corner. We can make it out of here as long as we are careful."

"You two are crazy," Ethen says. "I'm going back to the room. They are going to kill the two of you out here, and I want to be as far away as possible when that happens. If they come into the room, I will shoot them. That is the whole purpose of having a gun, right?" By the time Ethen ends his sentence, he is practically crying, and the pitch in his voice has gone up.

I give Aiden a quick, worried glance since I'm not sure I want to go with Ethen anywhere anymore. I'm afraid he is going to panic and get us killed.

Aiden stares at Ethen hard before grabbing Ethen by the shoulders, pushing him to the wall, and giving him a piece of his mind. "You don't have enough bullets. None of us do. You are a grown adult. Stop acting like a child. If you don't grow up right now, then we will all die. Do you not think we are scared, too? We are, but we are not showing it because right now is not the time to feel scared. We need to be calm so that we can think things through clearly and make reasonable decisions."

Aiden continues in a sedate voice, "If you want to be scared of something, be scared of me because right now, I am your biggest threat. I want to help you get out of here, I really do, but if you don't stop and get your shit together, then I will have to leave you here. Do you want that?" Ethen shakes his frightened head no. "Good. Then you are going to follow Sam and I, you are going to do as we say, and we are all going to get out of here alive. Got it?"

Ethen nods his head in understanding, and Aiden lets him go.

Aiden angrily stares at Ethen for another minute and then walks back down the pathway where we came from. We pass the kitchen again and move further down the dark path until we can't go any further since we are met by a fence with a red tarp over it, like the one around the perimeter of the carnival. Aiden looks at the fence that goes around the back of the kitchen. I try to think if there is a way to climb the fence, but I scratch that idea the second I look at Ethen.

It's not that I don't think he could climb a fence. I just don't think he could do it quietly and without panicking.

"I think we can fit through. There is just enough space for a person to move back here between the fence and the wall. We'll take this way until we get to the end of the building. Then there should be another spot of games along with another open space we can cross to get over to the other side of the carnival."

I take a quick look between the building and the fence, and I know that he is most likely right. We can fit as long as we walk sideways. Then, it looks like there are more games at the end that we could hide behind until we get to a spot where it is safe to cross over to the other side, where the Mirror Maze is. I notice that Aiden hasn't told Ethen about the Mirror Maze being our way out.

Ethen and I nod at Aiden in understanding, and then we each start making our way through. Aiden is in front once again. I'm behind him, and Ethen is behind me. We have to turn our bodies so that our backs are against the fence and we are facing the wall of the kitchen. After a few more feet, the wall to the kitchen ends, and there is about two feet of space between it and the next building, similar to how the game booths are.

We go one by one to the next building, and when I make it over, I quickly notice that there is less space behind here than behind the kitchen. When my back rubs against the tarp-covered fence, and I hear the sound of it creaking, I push myself as close to the building as possible so that it does not happen again.

I hear Ethen breathing heavily beside me, but I do my best to tune him out. I am not too good in small spaces, and if I listen to his rapid breathing and panicking, then I'm probably going to join him.

The last thing I want to do right now is to become like Ethen. Actually, the last thing I want to do right now is get caught, but becoming like Ethen is a close second.

When we reach the end of the building, Aiden gets out and moves behind one of the games. As I am getting out from behind the building to do the same thing, except I trip on a rock and have to use my hand to grab the corner of the building to make sure I don't fall. Once I'm standing normally again, I realize that something liquid-like and cold is on my hand. When I take my hand off the wall and put it in the small piece of light between where I'm standing and where the game in front of me is, I see that my hand is red.

"Why did you stop?" Ethen asks me in a whisper.

I look at Aiden, and he just says, "Don't look at it. We have to keep moving."

It's not the first time I have seen this much blood tonight, but I just can't seem to get used to the sight of it. Especially when it is on my hand.

I take a look to make sure there is no one coming before I cross the small piece of light and make it behind the same game booth that Aiden is behind. I wipe my hand against the back wall of the booth, trying to get the blood off. After that, I take a look to see Ethen doing the same thing Aiden and I just did. He looks for any guards, and when he is sure that the coast is clear, he joins us. The only difference between Ethen, and Aiden and I is that Ethen looked like he was going to throw up the whole time.

We stay behind the game for another minute as we hear the sound of a guard walking by. After the guard leaves, we don't say anything to each other since we don't want to attract unwanted attention. I am starting to find that I like the silence. It is peaceful and calming, not like the constant chatter I hear every time I walk outside my home.

Although I live somewhat apart from the rest of Treegrass, I can still hear the sound of kids yelling at one another from afar or the sound of adults talking to each other while taking a walk in the woods since my house is located at the end of the road and only a few feet into the woods.

Aiden peeks out from behind the game. He looks around the area and then comes back to our spot. He looks like he is thinking to himself for a minute before looking back at Ethen and me again.

"Okay, here is what is out there. This area is different from the area we crossed originally the first time," Aiden says to me, "while this one is wider, it's not as brightly lit up, and there are two different game booths that we can stop to hide inside while we make our way across. There is a fence with a torn up piece of cloth to the right about five hundred feet away, cutting this area off from the other area, but there is an opening that looks like a walkway, so we have to keep an eye on that."

I vividly remember what he is talking about. I think this is the area where Devin, my Dad, and I played the game that involved numbers and boxes. I think the fence Aiden is talking about was right behind that game. "Since the space is wider than the other one and the game booths are a little bigger, I think that we should move together. It will save time, and I think it will be better since it is relatively safe and it's darker than the other spot, so the guards are less likely to see us if we move quickly together. What are your thoughts?"

"Are you sure it's safer this way? What if they see us? Three people together are easier to see, and they make a bigger target. Shouldn't we go separately?" Ethen asks.

"I never thought I would say this, but Ethen has a point. It might take us longer to go separately, but I think it would be safer." I tell Aiden.

"I know. I know." Aiden looks across the area again and then back to us. "What if we go individually across to the first game booth, meet there, and then go separately across to the second game booth until we are together again, and then we go separately across to the other side? It's still relatively quick and safe."

"It sounds good to me," I tell Aiden. We then both look to Ethen

"Okay." He says reluctantly.

"Okay then," Aiden says, "I'll go first."

CHAPTER 24

Aiden looks to Ethen to see if he will object to Aiden going first, but when Ethen says nothing, Aiden checks to see if anyone is coming, and then he makes his way to the first booth.

Before Aiden reaches the booth, Ethen turns to me, "You trust him?" he asks.

I take a second to think about it before responding. "Yes," I tell him.

Once Aiden reaches the first game booth and makes sure no guards are coming, he waves for one of us to come over.

"Do you want to go next, or do you want me to?" I ask Ethen.

"I'll go," Ethen says.

Ethen pokes his head out from where we are hiding, looks to his right and then his left, and slowly moves to the booth. Midway there, his feet get faster, and he almost runs right into Aiden, but he stops himself at the last second.

While I cannot see Aiden's face all that well, I know he is sending death glares to Ethen. It will be a miracle if we manage to get out of here without Ethen doing something that will end up alerting a guard.

I wait for both boys to duck down further into the game booth before checking for any guards and making my way to the booth. Once I'm there, I crouch down and look at Aiden and Ethen.

"Be as quiet as possible. If this area is anything like the other one, then there should be a guard passing at any moment," Aiden says.

The three of us sit in silence for maybe thirty seconds before I hear the sound of footsteps coming our way. I know that Ethen hears it, too, because he looks at Aiden with panicked eyes. Aiden shoots Ethen an angry, threatening look, and Ethen's expression changes. Now, he looks like he is trying to act brave, but it looks more like he is in pain. His face starts turning red, and I realize he is holding his breath.

Once the sound of footsteps passes us and fades away, Ethen releases the breath of air he was holding in, and the red in his face slowly starts to disappear. More footsteps are heard in the distance, and when they start getting closer, the process on Ethen's face repeats.

I wonder if letting Ethen pass out will help us get out of here safer. Carrying an unconscious man out of here would probably be easier than having a conscious Ethen.

After a minute of silence, color returns to Ethens face, and Aiden slowly looks up from the booth. When he comes back down, he tells us that there are no guards coming at the moment. Aiden once again moves to make his way over to the second game booth, and Ethen once again sees that as an opportunity to ask me about Aiden.

"How do you know?" Ethen asks.

"How do I know I can trust him?" I ask Ethen, and he nods his head. "I know I can trust him because he saved me and my brother. He got us out of here, and then he was kind enough to bring me back in to try to find my Dad. He also promised my brother that he would bring me back alive, and I believe him when he says that he will."

Ethen does not ask anything else, and Aiden waves one of us over from the next booth.

"I trust him," I tell Ethen one more time with a hundred percent certainty in my words.

He does not say anything in response, he just looks to see if any guards are coming, and then he makes his way over to Aiden. I follow after him, and then the three of us repeat this process one more time until we are behind another row of games like Aiden and I were earlier when we first came back into the carnival. We get behind the game booth titled Water Bucket as Aiden takes a look around to try and determine if we should go right or left.

"I think if we go left, we'll get there quicker, and it should be relatively safe," Aiden says.

"Where is there?" Ethen asks, "You keep saying you're going to get me out of here, yet you fail to mention how we are going to do that. Do you know of some secret exit or something? Are we just going to walk right through the front gates of the carnival to get out of here?"

"We're going to get out of here. That's all that matters," Aiden says sternly.

I can tell Ethen does not like that answer, but I don't care. I don't trust him with the real one.

"You know you are a real asshole, right?" Ethen says in frustration.

"I may be an asshole, but I am a smart one. You don't need to know how to get out of here. You just have to trust that we will get you out," Aiden says back.

"Why would I trust you? I don't know anything about you."

"You know my name. You know where I am from. You don't know my personal life, but you do know my personality. I don't like people who complain. I also don't like people who freak out at the first sign of danger. It not only puts themselves at a greater risk of getting killed, but it also endangers the people around them."

"Fine," Ethen says, "as long as you get me out of here alive, I guess I shouldn't complain."

I don't believe that Ethen will stop complaining. He is too much like a little kid who just wants to get his way.

"You're right, you really shouldn't complain." Aiden says, "You should listen instead. Listen for any shooters, and listen to me when I say watch your step. There are a lot of wires back here, and they are easy to trip over or unplug, so I recommend you be careful."

The three of us start moving behind the game booths. Aiden is in front, I'm behind him, and Ethen is behind me. Every now and then, I hear Ethen mumbling to himself about the wires or the rubbery smell, but I try to ignore him and focus on where my own feet are going.

I hear Ethen fighting with the wires on the ground some more, but this time, he has to stop and untangle his foot before we are able to move again. We turn a corner and continue making our way to the maze.

I walk around the wires as if they are a minefield. Every time I look behind me, I see Ethen walking on top of the wires and accidentally looping his foot up in one as he walks. I try to tell Ethen to walk to the left side, where there are fewer wires, but he doesn't listen.

"I shouldn't be much farther," Aiden says quietly to me. "Is Ethen bothering you?"

"No. He keeps talking to himself about our situation. It is annoying, but I can put up with it."

"Let me know if you want to trade places," Aiden says while looking behind me at Ethen.

"Okay, stop. I need help," Ethen says.

"Of course you do," I say as I turn around and see that Ethen's foot is once again caught up in a bundle of wires.

"I think I accidentally tightened it when I tried getting it off."

"Let me see it," Aiden says.

Aiden walks over to Ethen and starts pulling at the wires. I hear more complaining from Ethen, and I can't help but laugh a little bit.

"You think this is funny?" says Ethen.

I look at Ethen's face and bluntly tell him, "Yes."

I hear Aiden laugh a little as well, and then he asks Ethen to lift his foot up a little more. After another thirty seconds, Aiden says, "Sam, can you please make sure no one is coming?"

"Why does she have to check to see if anyone is coming? You are not going to leave me here, are you? You can't do that to me!" Ethen starts pulling his leg up harder, but all that seems to do is tighten the wires around his foot.

"I'm not going to leave you here, but I do think that I have to unplug the game in order to get you untangled. If I do that and someone is walking by, then they might get suspicious and come over here. You don't want that, do you? No? Great, now shut up, and Sam, please make sure no one is coming." I can't help but smile at Aidens words and the monotone way he says them to Ethen.

I do as Aiden says, look between the two booths in front of me, and see no guards coming from any direction.

"All clear," I tell Aiden.

"Okay," Aiden says, putting his hand on the wire to pull it from the wall.

"Wait! What if-" Ethen's words get cut off when Aiden pulls the wire, and the lights to the game booth we are behind turn off.

Ethen goes silent and closes his eyes, and Aiden finishes getting his foot out.

"Done," Aiden says.

Ethen gets both of his feet back on the ground and free from any wires. "Well then, let's go."

We continue walking along the same way we were going before. We make another turn, walk a little longer, and then Aiden stops us. I look up at him, and he mouths the word guard. I nod in response, and then I look over to Ethen, who looks confused. Ethen opens his mouth to ask a question, but I quickly put one finger over my lips to signal to him to be quiet.

We are all quiet for a few seconds, and there is no noise. There is no sound of footsteps, no sound of movement, nothing.

After another minute, Ethan asks, "What are we waiting for?"

Aiden looks at Ethen with wide eyes. Ethen didn't even whisper those words. He might as well as shouted them for the guard to hear.

"Who's there?" Asks an unfamiliar male voice.

A head sticks out from around the corner of the booth, and Aiden quickly grabs my hand. "Run!" He shouts.

Aiden pulls my hand to go around the side of the game booth opposite the guard's. I look at Ethen and see his foot is stuck in another set of wires.

"Wait, you can't leave without me! Please! Stop! Please!" Ethen Yells to us, "You can't leave me here! You can't!"

Ethen tries to break free of the wire, but he falls to the floor instead. He then tries to fire his gun at the guard but misses. The guard easily knocks the gun out of his hand and moves to grab Ethen. The guard then grabs his walkie-talkie and starts talking into it.

"We need to go! Now Sam!"

Aiden pulls my hand, and we start running.

I hear the guard's voice yelling in the distance. "I'm in the southeast plaza. They're heading west. Send more..."

Chapter 25

We keep moving at a constant pace. It is a good thing I am used to racing Devin because it has really helped me practice for tonight.

We keep running and running and running, just trying not to get caught.

As I make my way past them, the booths turn to blur. The vibrant glow they once had turns into smooth, thin lines of vague colors that I can no longer remember the names of.

All that consumes my mind is Devin. I need to make it back to him alive. I might be the only family member he has left still breathing. I need to get out of here and away from these guards, and I know the only way I can do that is with Aiden's help.

Every now and then, Aiden pulls my arm to steer me to the right or to the left, and I don't question him. My heart is racing, and I am almost out of breath. I keep telling myself that it's just a little further. I just have to make it a few more feet, and then everything will be alright.

I know it's not true, but I need to keep moving. Wherever Aiden is taking us can't possibly be much farther, right? There are only so many places where a person could run to.

I know that we have run in a circle a few times. I don't know if this is to confuse the guards or something, but I don't bother asking Aiden. Whatever he is doing is working. With each turn we make, there are fewer guards behind us. I keep looking over my shoulder every few minutes to see how many guards there are, or in other words, I look to see how much danger we are in.

At the start of this, there were only two, then there were five, and at the height of it, there were eight since we ran past one of those small rooms I was in earlier, and there were still guards outside of it. Now though, with Aiden's weird but useful tactic of taking random turns and running in circles, there are only three behind us.

We are both running at top speed, and every now and then, Aiden has to tell me when we will make a sudden turn. He tells me when we should go right or left, and how he says it makes me believe that he memorized this whole carnival.

For all I know, he could just be guessing what direction we should go in. I don't think he could really have memorized the whole layout of the place since he had to think about what direction we should go in when we were with Ethen. He must have remembered the way the carnival was in Tundris and figured that the carnivals were set up the same everywhere.

The governors probably figured they could make all the carnivals the same since it would make moving the carnival to the next town easier. They probably didn't think about the possibility of people escaping the carnivals and breaking back in when they moved to another town.

I glance behind us. A handful of guards are still chasing us, but two of them are much faster than the others. "They are gaining on us," I tell Aiden.

"We will lose them," Aiden says. "Just keep moving! Another left"

Just as we start to turn left, I see two guards come running at us. "Not left!" I say quickly.

Aiden pulls my hand, and we backtrack our steps and take off in a new direction.

"Left," he says right as he pulls my arm left down the main entrance plaza. We make another turn left and start running past all the game booths. We run a few more feet before he says left again, and we are running through the food area with all the tables and chairs laid out.

The place looks kind of eerie since I could practically see all the faces of the people who were having a good time earlier before the government started to kill people. I look behind us to see two guards left.

"Right," he says, and in that instant, we both turn right down an alleyway. The second we make the turn, we both start backing up and running back in the direction we were running before.

Down that alleyway, there are a whole group of guards. We try to make another turn out of the food court, but another group of guards turns us around. I don't bother turning around to see how many are behind us now. There is no doubt in my mind that they are catching up to us.

All the guards I thought we lost behind us apparently just grouped together. I have no idea how many guards there are in this whole carnival, but if there are more guard groups like that behind another corner or turn, then Aiden and I are screwed.

"What do we do?" I ask Aiden in a panic.

"I don't know! Just keep running!"

We try to run for the small entryway that leads to another section of games, but more guards turn us around once again.

The two of us run in another direction and take off towards one of the last ways out. There is a decently large opening between the guard surrounded area we are currently in and the other side of the carnival. We start running that way just as guards come in from that direction. I start to slow my run so that we can turn around and look for another way out, but Aiden apparently has other plans. He keeps pulling my arm in that direction anyway.

"We can make it," he says. "I think we can make it. Just keep running!"

I understand what he is saying. The guards coming in from that direction are not moving that fast, and if we run fast enough and stick to the left side of the wall, we might be able to run past them and get out of this guard-infested part of the carnival.

I look at Aiden and see the determination on his face. He really believes we can do it. I try to force my legs to go faster. If we do make it, then it will be by a hair.

We get closer and closer, and I think the guards start to realize what we are planning on doing because they start moving faster towards the little open gap as well. As we are running through, a guard reaches out and grabs my arm. I am instantly yanked back and I let go of Aiden's hand. I tug my arm free of the guard and kick him in the shin. I claw at his hand, and his grip loosens. I manage to free myself from him and avoid the other arms reaching for me.

More guards start moving in. I push past a guard, but they get too close, and I can't fight them all.

One grabs me from behind, while another comes at me. I kick my legs at the guard that is holding me in the hopes of him letting go. There is the sound of a gunshot, and my blood runs cold.

Did they shoot me? I don't feel any pain.

I feel the guard's grip on me loosen, and I see Aiden start pushing guards out of the way while waving his gun at them. I manage to break free from the guard, and once I do, Aiden motions to start running again.

Aiden grabs my hand once again and starts running with me. He definitely could have run off without me, but he didn't. He probably should have since that could have ended very badly for the both of us, but I am glad he didn't.

We take off running full speed ahead with the guards right behind us. The guards are getting closer to us, and I don't know how much longer we can run before they catch us. Right after Aiden and I make a quick right turn, Aiden lets go of my hand and grabs hold of his gun once more.

The lack of pain I feel must mean that he was the one who shot the gun before. I don't know where he aimed it, but it helped us get out of there.

I hear the sound of his gun going off, but I am too afraid to turn around and look. I slow down my running pace a little bit so that Aiden can catch up with me, and he does. We take off running at full speed again until the sound of the guards gets closer. Aiden does what he did before and slows down his pace so that he can shoot at some of the guards.

This time, I take a look behind us and see that he is aiming for their legs. This makes me feel a little better since I am not sure if I would be able to handle the death of so many people in one day. I also don't know if I could live with myself knowing that I played a hand in another person's death. The guards might not be the best people in the world, but they are still people nonetheless. I also don't feel good about Aiden or me killing someone who isn't even shooting at us.

But then again, all the people who died here in Treegrass today and in Tundris a little while back also didn't have guns or weapons, and yet the government had the guards kill them. This is all just an awful situation.

Aiden stops shooting, and we speed up our pace again. The shooting has luckily caused us to gain a little distance from the guards. I take a quick glance back and see that there are still many guards running after us, probably about fifteen to twenty. Not that I am complaining, but I really don't understand why they don't shoot at one of our legs. They need to catch us alive in order to find the others, and they have guns, so why don't they use them?

We run straight for a while before Aiden decides that we should go left. Once we make the turn, we could either go straight down and make a right or make another left. Instead of either of those options, Aiden grabs my hand again and leads the two of us towards a game booth. Once inside, Aiden crouches down, and I do the same. The two of us move as far back into the booth as we can and wait to hear the sound of the guards running by.

As the sound of the guards gets closer, I instinctively push myself as far into the booth as possible, although I know that a guard running by would not see me or Aiden in here.

I look at Aiden as we wait to hear the guards leave. He is out of breath, just like I am. We look at each other for what feels like an eternity before the sound starts to fade again. Neither of us says anything after it gets quiet. We just continue to look at each other until our breathing slows down.

Chapter 26

Every now and then, there are more footsteps heard running by us, and from the sound of things, it seems like the guards have split up again. I wait another minute before silently asking Aiden if he is good to go, and by silently asking, I mean by giving him hand signals of me pointing at him, giving him a thumbs up, and then pointing out the booth. He seems to get my message and proceeds to wait until it is quiet again before peeking his head out from around the bottom of the booth.

Aiden slowly stands up and reaches out his hand for mine. I take it, and together, we start cautiously walking around the area. We make a few more turns and find ourselves right back near the entrance. How many times have we been here today?

We move to walk behind the game booths, where it is a little darker, and I let Aiden lead the way since he seems to have a better memory of the layout than I do. We have to stop walking a few times to let the guards pass, but ultimately, I think we are doing pretty good, considering just a few minutes ago, we had a whole army of guards behind us.

When we are able to move again, we get about ten feet before we end up making a right turn around a corner. We move quietly to get behind the first booth, then the second booth, and then the third one.

As Aiden and I are about to cross over behind the fourth booth, a guard's head sticks out from behind two booths. His head is about three booths away and is currently looking away from us. Fear courses through my veins. Before I could even think to move, his head turns to look to his left, and he looks directly at us.

Aiden pulls us back the way we came, and we start running again. I don't look back behind us to see if the guard is chasing us because I already know he is. Of course, he is. Aiden and I are practically enemy number one in their book, and they just won't leave us alone.

We continue running, and as we make more turns, we are seen by more guards, and the number of people running after us grows again. Aiden lets out a series of curse words and then leads us right, left, and left again. After that, we gained some distance from the guards, and I catch sight of the next place we could hide for a little while until the guards spread out again.

I give Aiden's hand a tug and point to the rock wall. He nods his head in agreement, and we both run to hide behind it before the guards catch up to us and see where we are going. Once behind the wall, I realize that this might not have been the best idea. There are a lot of big leafy bushes behind the wall.

"Too late to change our minds now. The shooters will be here any minute. I think we should get in the bushes," Aiden says.

I know he is right, so I cover my face with my arms and lower myself into one bush. Branches poke at me, and leaves hit me in the face as Aiden comes to sit down in the bush next to me. This is definitely not an ideal situation, but I guess it could be worse.

I hear the sound of running feet go by, and I wait a minute after that to speak.

"What do we do now?" I whisper to Aiden through the leaves.

He looks at me, but he looks exhausted. "I don't know."

After another minute, I decide to ask another question that has been on my mind. "When Ethen gave away where we were to the guards, why did we run away from the maze? We weren't that far away from it. Why didn't you want to run that way?"

"I didn't want to give our plan away," Aiden says. "If we ran that way and didn't make it to the maze, then they would have found out that we were trying to go that way, and the maze would have at least ten guards standing outside it by now if we did."

He takes a short pause before speaking again. "Anyway, if we managed to make it to the maze and get out of the carnival, they would have chased us into the woods and found out where we were hiding. It just wouldn't have ended well, so I figured we should run in the opposite direction."

I nod my head in understanding. If we were to have run to where Theon and the other Jumpers are in the woods with Devin and all the other Treegrass people, then we would have been putting them in danger. We could have accidentally given away their location, and the guards could have sent all their men out to hunt them down and capture them. What they would do after they caught them, I have no clue. Would they kill them, or would they let the people who originally had the green light live?

I think about what Aiden said earlier about the people who didn't go to the carnival. People who didn't go to the carnival could be seen as defying the government's wishes and killed. If Devin or I were to be caught by the guards, I have no doubt in my mind that they would kill us, too, since we didn't do what they wanted us to.

But how could we? There was no way anyone would willingly let their family or friends die just because the New World said that they should. I don't care if the New World is having problems. As long as I have my family, I would not mind the hardships.

Even now, if I had to give up my house and live in a bush, I would do it as long as I had my family, and I knew that there were people out there who were doing the best they could to fix whatever problems came our way. But I no longer know if I have my parents or my house. All I know is that I am sitting in a bush because the stupid New World government made the wrong choice.

I want to make them pay, but how? The people who are doing this live far away and have the best military. Even if we went around town to town and rescued everyone, we still wouldn't be able to stop the people in the town of Officials.

I wonder what the Jumpers are really like. Are they all like Aiden, Theon, and Vesper? Do they really want to help all the towns escape the deadly carnivals? What is their plan after that if they succeed? There are just too many questions and not enough answers.

"What is the plan after the carnivals? I mean, what will the Jumpers do after they rescue everyone?" I ask.

Aiden doesn't answer right away. "I don't know. We haven't thought that far ahead yet. We have just been taking it one day at a time so far."

I guess that answers all right. They weren't prepared for something like this to happen. There was no plan. "Were you really going to let Ethen join us? That guy clearly wasn't in his right mind. He wished his own brothers dead," I tell Aiden.

Aiden thinks about it for a moment. "Yes," he says, "just because someone thinks or believes something today doesn't mean they will tomorrow. People change, and although Ethen might not be the most sane person I have ever met, it does not mean that he can't change over time." After a brief pause, he says, "So yes, I would have brought him with us."

After that, I kind of feel like a jerk for asking. Of course, people can change. No one is born to be just one way in life. On top of that, Ethen has probably had just as bad of a day as I have, and we are just handling it in two different ways.

I wonder where Ethen is. Did the guards take him away to interrogate him about our whereabouts, or did they kill him after realizing that he does not have much information about us since we didn't tell him anything too important?

I feel something crawling up my leg, and I try to swipe at it with my hand.

"Try not to think about it," Aiden says.

"That is easier said than done, especially when you're in a bush surrounded by creepy crawly things that are gross and disgusting." I stare at my legs and arms, trying to catch the sight of anything on me that I can smack off.

"They're not going to hurt you," Aiden says with some amusement in his voice.

I grew up surrounded by bugs and insects. I have a brother who never let me forget about their existence. Just because I am used to them doesn't mean I like them or want them crawling all over me.

I give him an angry look, but unfortunately, I don't think he could see it in the dark behind multiple bush branches. "I know they won't hurt me. That is not the problem. The problem is that there are creepy, crawly, disgusting things crawling up my legs and arms. Sorry, but I'm not very happy about it."

I think I hear Aiden laugh a little, but I ignore him. I am too tired to argue or fight. I just want to go home and go to bed. I think today's events are finally catching up with my body because it feels like I have just worked out for six hours straight. My feet hurt, my legs are tired, my lungs are on fire and I am pretty sure my brain stopped functioning sometime during the chase.

I hear footsteps come walking towards us, and I hope they walk away soon. The footsteps get closer, and I start to hear the sound of static on the guard's walkie-talkie. I see a light shining our way, and I close my eyes. I'm done fighting. I'm too tired. If the guard sees me, he could have me, but he is going to have to kill me because I am not telling him anything about anyone.

I hear the static sound again and then the guard's voice, "All clear over here. Has anyone checked back over at the front?"

His voice, along with his footsteps, get further away, and I let out a breath of air. He must not have seen us in the bushes. The leaves probably covered us. I open my eyes again and see the familiar darkness.

"Okay," Aiden says once the guard walks away, "I think I know what we should do now."

"What's your plan?"

CHAPTER 27

"**W**ell, if I remember correctly, then we are on the completely opposite side of the maze. We are now back over by the two rooms and the main tent, which means that we could try and go back the same way we got over here last time when we were trying to get into the rooms, or we could try going a different route," Aiden says.

I remember how the one guard looked behind the games as Aiden and I were walking behind them, "I think the guards are starting to catch onto our method of moving behind the games. What's the other route?"

"The other route we could take is one I have not gone before. In Tundris, we ran away from the tent just like you guys did, and now I am starting to wonder what is over there on the other side of it," Aiden says, his voice tinged with a mix of curiosity and apprehension. "Every time the guards have spotted us, it has been by games, so maybe we try something different and see if there is a way out over by the main tent where there are no games."

I think about what Aiden is saying. Since we have been seen near the game booths before, the guards are probably going to check them more thoroughly, and we will most likely get caught. The main tent, on the other hand, is where we ran from and is guarded in the front and most likely on the side facing the Ferris wheel as well since that was where another entrance was, so maybe the guards won't think to look for us behind it.

If there is a way out from behind the tent, we could get out of here and back to the group sooner since the main tent is closer to where we are than the maze.

"Okay, and if there is no way out from there, then we can go back to the game booths," I tell Aiden. "And if there are a bunch of guards back there, then we will continue running around this place like mice getting chased by cats."

"Exactly," Aiden says, his voice filled with determination and a hint of eagerness.

"Great," I say with not much enthusiasm.

Aiden gives me a little smile and then moves to stand up. I stand up as well, but I try to brush all the dirt, leaves, and bugs off of myself while I am doing it. I am really not much of a bug person, and I would like to get away from them as soon as possible.

We move to the edge of the rock wall, and I peer out from the side to look at our surroundings. It has definitely gotten darker, but I can still make out the Go Fishing game next to us, along with a little outline of the first building I went in off in the distance.

"The main tent should be straight ahead," I tell Aiden.

I check to make sure no guards are coming before I move out from behind the wall and make my way to the fishing game. Once there, I quickly look around at the inside of the game. This is one of the games I won earlier today. We had to use little toy fishing poles with magnets on the ends to catch toy fish in the water. Whoever could catch the most fish within a minute won. I remember the game looking pretty since it had a painted background that showed the bright blue ocean. Now, the ocean looks dark and depressing. The contrast between the game's cheerful facade and the grim reality of our situation is stark, and it sends a chill down my spine.

I move behind the game, and Aiden joins me a few seconds later. Now, we are right back where we were earlier, trying to figure out how to get into the first room to find what Vesper saw. There are still guards walking around, but fewer than before. They must all be looking for Aiden and me elsewhere.

The lights outside the buildings are still on, and every few minutes, there are one or two guards going in and out of one of the buildings. I wonder what they are doing in there. The first room does not have as many people moving in and out of it. From what I remember, it just looked like some sort of break room where they used to sit down and relax when they got too tired or hungry. The other room is the opposite, that was the room with all the papers in it, there is a lot more activity going on in it now. Luckily, building two is on the far side away from us, and I think we can make it to the left side of building one without being seen if we move quickly enough.

Aiden and I look over the game booth and watch the guards who go in, out, and around the buildings. If there is some sort of pattern, then we should use that to our advantage. From what I can tell, a guard walks by the two buildings every minute or so, and they tend to come from the right and move toward our direction, but they don't check the game booths over here. The unpredictability of the guards' movements adds to the challenge of getting out of here.

The guards going in and out of the first room are not very frequent—maybe every three or four minutes. The guards in the second room are definitely more active and move around more. There is a guard going in or out of the room every thirty seconds or so.

A guard walks by us, and fifteen seconds later, another guard comes out of the second room. Since a guard walked into the first room only about a minute ago, I figure this is our best time to move.

I grab Aiden's hand, my pulse racing as we swiftly move to the side of building one. The area is brighter, forcing me to squint until my eyes adjust. By the time we reach the side of the building, my heart is pounding in my chest. I press myself against the wall, acutely aware that the main tent is only a few feet away, heavily guarded. I fix my gaze on the chain link fence wall covered in a red tarp, trying to push away the thoughts of getting caught.

I can't bear the thought of letting Devin down.

We have been in here for probably about two hours at least. We were just supposed to get to the room, find the list of the towns, and look for my Dad along the way. That should only have taken about thirty minutes, an hour at most, but definitely not two or more hours. Every minute that passes, the risk of getting caught increases, and the urgency of our task to get out of here becomes more apparent.

Devin is probably worried about me, and I am starting to feel bad about leaving him out there alone. When the sun begins to come up, the Jumpers will leave with all the people from Treegrass who they got out, but I know that Devin won't leave without me. If I'm not there, then he is not leaving, which means that I have to make it there.

I slowly move my head so that I can just see over the edge of the building to where the main tent is. There are still four guards standing out front like before, but I think we can get to the side of the tent by moving from tree to tree.

Some of the trees here are tall and have branches that start growing from about eight to ten feet high, like the maple and varnish trees. Others, like the yellow birch and the box elder maple tree, have branches that hang lower to the ground. These are the types of trees that would be the most ideal for us to hide behind since their leaves could help cover us.

The first tree is a maple, and its trunk is wide enough for one of us to be behind it at a time without being seen. The first tree is about four or five feet away, so I look to see where the guards at the front of the tent are looking. From here, it is hard to tell exactly where they are looking, but since their heads are facing straight forward, I assume their eyes are looking there as well.

When I feel confident enough, I make the short distance to the tree. Once there, I move my body to make sure the guards at the tent can't see me. I look over to Aiden and see that he is standing in the same spot I was before. I can't tell what he is thinking, but he does not seem scared or worried about what we are doing.

I look to make sure the guards haven't seen me, and then I make my way to the second tree, which is only a few strides away. Once I make it there, I look over to Aiden to see that he is starting to move over to the first tree. When he makes it there, he leans his right shoulder against the tree trunk and faces me. He gives me a small nod to let me know that we're good.

I turn my back to him and move to the third tree. Since there is not much distance between the trees here, I am less worried about being caught. I then move from behind one tree to the next, checking to make sure the guards are still looking straight ahead each time. I don't have to look behind me to know that Aiden is following. I can hear his feet shuffling on the ground. It is quiet enough that no one outside a ten-foot radius could hear it.

I make the last few steps to the main tent and stay on the side of it so that none of the guards can see me. Aiden joins me a few seconds later, and once there, neither of us says anything for a minute.

Chapter 28

Aiden stares at me like he is trying to figure something out. He does not say anything, but I can tell something is on his mind.

I am the first to speak. "What?" I ask him.

"Nothing," he says and turns to start walking towards the back of the tent.

"What, I want to know."

"You're going to get mad at me."

I can't help but laugh a little, "Well, now I have to know."

He stops walking and turns around to face me. "I just thought you would be more scared. I saw the look on your face when I was bringing you and your townspeople over to the maze to get you guys out. You looked terrified. You even looked scared when you were asking me to help you get back in. I don't see any of that fear now."

When I don't respond, he keeps going. "It's not a bad thing you're no longer scared. I was just noticing." He says awkwardly, like he wants to stop talking, although he continues anyway. "I know girls don't like being called scared since most people assume scared means weak, and I didn't want you to think I was calling you weak. Fear is what keeps many people alive, and fear can make people do amazing things. I'm scared all the time. Please don't be mad."

"I'm not mad," I tell him.

I'm not. He's right. Fear is a good thing. I was scared before, but I'm also scared right now. Apparently, I just got good at hiding it. Or maybe I am too exhausted to care about anything like fear right now.

I am not even scared of the guards anymore. I am more scared of not making it back to Devin. I promised him I would come back, and I do not intend on breaking that promise.

Most of all, I am scared of not finding my Dad, but most of all, I am afraid of finding him dead. I know we have not had time to look for him in every booth since we have been running from the guards, but I am terrified that I am going to turn a corner, and he is going to be laying on the ground lifeless.

"Is this one of those things where someone says they're not mad, but they really are, and you are going to get me back for it later?" Aiden says.

I snap out of my thoughts. "No," I tell him with a slight smile on my face.

"Okay, if you say so. But just in case you are lying, you should know that I know a cop. If you try anything, he will find you." Aiden says to me with a sideways glance so I can see the smile on his face that tells me he is joking.

We start walking again along the side of the show tent until we come to the area where my Dad, Devin, and I, along with a few others, broke out from. The spot now has a long piece of wood covering the opening. On top of the wood lies a section of the tarp that is now ripped in many places and has a few holes that look to be from bullets. Light shines through parts of the tarp that does not have wood behind it, and I am tempted to look in and see if I recognize anyone in there.

I point to the hole in the tarp, and Aiden understands what I am asking. He gets closer to it, peeks in, and then comes back to stand beside me. I can tell by the grim look on his face that it's not good.

"If you want to look inside, you can, but you might not want to." He says to me in a whisper.

"I want to," I tell him. There is no changing my mind about it. Maybe there is a small chance that my Dad ended up in there somewhere, and they didn't kill him.

"Alright. Just be careful. There is a circle of shooters in the center. Each of them is holding a gun, and if they spot you, there is a good chance they won't hesitate to shoot you," Aiden tells me.

I give him a nod of understanding, and then I approach the small hole in the tarp. I slowly peek in and look to the center to make sure none of the guards are looking my way.

As Aiden said, they are all in the middle of the room, standing in a circle facing the people sitting down on the bleachers. One look at the big guns that each of the guards holds reminds me of why Aiden and Theon call them shooters and not guards. They look ready to shoot anyone who looks at them the wrong way. They are definitely not the usual guards that I have seen come into town.

When I am certain that the guards can't see me, I start looking around at the room. There is so much red around the room that it makes the whole tent glow red. The bright lights that line the inside of the tent and the bottom of the bleachers seem out of place compared to all the blood and the somber faces of the people inside.

I see my neighbors, Jake, Leia, and Mike Populus, but Michelle Populus is not sitting with them. I look around the tent, but I can not find her. I look at all the faces of the people who have lived in Treegrass with me my whole life, but I am only able to remember a few of their names—some people I don't recognize at all.

Some people are crying, some are sitting staring at the guards in fear, and other people look like ghosts of themselves. They sit on the bleachers with blank expressions on their faces and are looking at nowhere in particular. Almost everyone has some blood on them. It is hard to find someone who does not. Some people are covered in blood, while others just have a few spots here and there.

What happened here after we ran out?

There is a pool of blood directly on the other side of the tarp where I am standing. The guards must have opened fired on everyone who was running out of the tent. There are other spots of blood around the room in various sizes. Some of the blood is smeared on the ground as if the person bleeding was being dragged away.

Regardless of all the blood, there are no bodies. As far as I can tell, the people being held in the tent aren't even injured. Did the guards take the injured people away to get medical help, or did they kill them as well?

I look around the tent to see if I can see my Dad anywhere. I know it's a long shot, but I have to try. If he somehow managed to get in here, then I can't leave without him. I look at every face in this room, but I don't see him. While there are many faces in here that are dirty or bloody, they don't look like him.

I quickly look over to the shooters again and then walk back over to Aiden. "Okay, we can go now," I tell him. I try to sound unbothered, but I'm not. My Dad's not here. He's not with the group back in the woods, and he's not here in the carnival. That means he's dead.

I avoid looking Aiden in the eyes since I don't want him to see me upset, but I don't think it works. Aiden grabs my hand and slowly starts leading me further along the outside of the main tent until we come to the end.

At the end, we should be able to make a right turn to continue our way, but we can't. The fence with the tarp over it extends to block this part off. We can't get through this way.

I can hear the sound of people walking around on the other side, and I look at Aiden questionably. The noise seems to make Aiden interested as well, and he leans in closer to the makeshift wall to listen, and I do the same. I can hear the hum of a vehicle and the sound of something being placed down hard on some sort of surface.

I look down to the bottom of the tarp and see that it's not connected to anything. I get down on the ground, and Aiden joins me after noticing this. I pick the tarp up and slowly start lifting it a few inches.

On the other side of the fence, there are hundreds or even thousands of body bags lying on the ground. If what the government said was true about killing half the population in Treegrass, then there are probably close to six thousand dead bodies here, maybe more.

The lighting is poor, but I can make out the bodies lying on the ground further to the right. Those bodies are not yet in bags. I can see that the guards are working to put those bodies in bags and with the others. I can't help but stare at them. I can see the faces of the people before the guards zip up the bags. Most have their eyes closed, but some are wide open, staring lifelessly at nothing.

To the left, there are guards loading the body bags onto a big truck. One by one, they load them on, and each time they put another one on, I can hear the sound of the body hitting the bed of the truck. They don't even bother to put them down gently. They just throw them on top of one another as if they mean nothing. One after another after another after another.

Thunk thunk thunk thunk.

I can't take it anymore. I let go of the tarp and lay on the ground. I try to focus on the stars in the sky and not the repeated sound of dead bodies being zipped up or thrown on a truck, but I can't get the sound out of my ears.

Thunk thunk thunk thunk.

Chapter 29

I can't feel anything.

I know that Aiden gets me to my feet, but I can't feel it. My body is numb but moving with help from Aiden. He helps me walk along the tent back to where we came from. We pass the boarded-up part of the tent but stop a little before the spot where we crossed from the trees.

"Sam, are you okay?" I stare at Aiden, but all I see is the guards putting people in body bags and throwing them in a pile, where more guards pick them up and throw them in a truck.

I don't respond to his question. I'm not okay. None of this is okay. My Dad's body is probably in one of those body bags being tossed around as if he means nothing to anyone. He is everything to me. If he is indeed dead, then he deserves a proper funeral. Everyone does.

What they are doing isn't right. None of it is. How do they live with themselves knowing that they have taken away people's grandparents, mothers, fathers, brothers, sisters, and friends? How do they expect people to listen to them after this? Everyone in the

New World, including myself, will never be able to trust them ever again.

"Sam, can you hear me?" Aiden asks. I am practically leaning all my weight on him, but he doesn't let me fall. His hand is on my face, but I can barely feel it.

The sound of the bodies hitting the ground still rings in my ears, although we have put distance between ourselves and that spot. "They killed them," Is all I manage to say. It comes out quieter than a whisper, but I know he hears me. "They killed all of them."

Aiden holds me tighter, "I know."

"They just killed them. For what? I don't understand." If the New World is experiencing problems and there really is no good solution, then at least kick them out and put them in no man's land. At least give them a chance at living.

The more I think about it, the more I understand why the New World would never do that. If they kicked people out, then those people could fight to get back in, and we would be at war all over again. Considering people in the towns would probably help their family members and friends who were kicked out, the New World would never win, so they would never choose that option.

Instead, they decided to kill. They chose to kill innocent people who had no idea what was going to happen to them tonight.

I think about my Dad and how I would have done anything for him to be here with me right now. I can't help but wonder if he is with my Mom. Are they at least together in death? Are they even dead? Is there some way that my Mom could be alright? What if Devin and I are the only two members of our family left?

I don't want the last memory of my Dad to be of him tackling two guards down so that Devin and I could run away. I know that everyone is going to die one day. I was just hoping that when he did, it would be from old age and lying on a bed peacefully. I think about what he said before he ran at the guards. He said he loved us.

Another minute goes by before I can start to feel my body again. "He's dead. They killed him. I didn't even get to say goodbye." I can't help myself, tears start running down my face, and I don't stop them.

Aiden manages to wipe away my tears while still holding me. Fresh tears replace the ones he wipes away, but he does not stop. The two of us just stand there on the side of the tent. I'm trying to hold my mouth in order to muffle the sound of my crying while Aiden holds me and tries to calm me down.

When I regain control of my tears, I am able to ask the question I have been wondering about since I first saw the bodies. "How did they die?" I don't expect Aiden to know, but I ask him anyway.

"What do you mean?" He asks.

"I mean, they weren't shot," I tell him. My voice breaks as I speak, but I continue anyway, "Yes, a few of them had blood on them, but many did not. I watched them put the bodies in the bags. There were no signs of any wounds on them. So how did they die?"

Aiden doesn't say anything for a few minutes, but when he does, it's just to say, "I don't know."

We stand there in silence for a while before I decide to say something. "When Devin and I were little, my Dad would take us over to the park after he got done with work. He would take us over to a small lake where we would sit there all day and listen to him tell us stories. When we got older, we started telling him stories that we made up. Our stories didn't make much sense, but he would listen anyway." I don't know why I tell him this, but I do.

"When we would get back home, we would find our Mom sitting there on the porch making a blanket. We would sit by her and help her pick out different colors. We would even get paper and markers and start drawing the designs that we thought she should do next. After I started high school, I stopped going to the park as much with my Dad and Devin. I even stopped picking out colors for my Mom. I would still play games with Devin, but I started to ignore my parents. I'm a terrible daughter."

"No, you are not," Aiden tells me. "That's just what kids do. They grow up and want independence. It doesn't make you a bad daughter. It just makes you human."

"But I am a bad daughter," I tell him. "My Dad wanted me to be an architect just like his father, and I wanted that too. I took the classes for it. I even took the placement test to determine if I would be accepted for an apprenticeship. I got it. I was the first female in our town to get an architect apprenticeship. When I found out, I was so happy. I knew my Dad would be happy, too, considering he helped me study for it. He stayed up with me all night when I couldn't figure something out. He wouldn't give me the answers to my problems, but he would give me words of encouragement and ask me to retrace my steps in order to figure out what I did wrong."

Aiden loosens his hold on me in order to look at me better. "I turned down the apprenticeship," I tell him. "I don't even know why I did it. I was scared, I guess. I couldn't even tell my Dad the truth. I lied to him and told him that I didn't get it. He was so mad. I had to spend the rest of the week preventing him from going to the school and yelling at the teachers. I became a house cleaner instead. To this day, I can't tell if I made the right decision or if I regret it."

Aiden lets go of me and sits down on the ground. I do the same.

It has just been too long of a day to continue standing when it feels like the world is crashing down all around.

"I wish my parents cared that much about me. I never had that kind of relationship with my Mom or Dad. They were always working all the time, and when they were home, they favored my oldest brother Dixon." Aiden says after I am done venting about my own father. "I didn't mind my parents giving him all the attention. When they were looking at him, it meant that they weren't looking at me. I got away with a whole lot. I also didn't get away with a lot. I was never proud of my Dad, and I'm still not, especially now, but I do care for my other older brother, Alex, and my younger sister, Autumn. I don't know where they are now, but I hope they're doing alright."

"They are not with you and the Jumpers?" I ask him.

Aiden is silent. He gives me a quick glance, then shakes his head no.

I decide it is a good time to change the topic. This is getting too depressing. "Why are you guys called the Jumpers anyway?" It's been a question on my mind since Aiden and Theon first mentioned it. "Do you guys like jumping around all day like rabbits or something?"

Aiden smiles slightly at that, "No. We are not called Jumpers for jumping around like rabbits," he says mimicking me. "Back in Tundris, our houses and apartments were built kind of high up, so when it snowed, a whole lot of people could still see the buildings.

Since we would get anywhere from eight to twenty feet of snow during the winter time, it was hard to go outside."

"A few years back," he says, "someone found out that if you make an entranceway on your roof, then you would just have to shovel your roof, and then you can jump from one building to the next since most of them were close enough together. Jumping from roof to roof became the best form of travel in the winter, and some people would even do it in the summer." The way he says the last part makes me think he was one of the ones who jumped rooftops all year long.

"Houses, apartments, and almost every work building were located close to each other, which just encouraged us to jump more." Aiden continues, "As I said before, though, many of the houses and buildings were not made right. While jumping from roof to roof was fun and all, it was also dangerous since you never knew if you would be jumping onto solid ground or if the roof was going to fall through."

"Anyway though, when we ran away from Tundris after the carnival, we were all sitting around one night, and somehow we got talking about the New World. We decided that we didn't want to be associated with them anymore, so we came up with a new name for ourselves. While we are not our own country or anything, we figured calling ourselves the Jumpers would separate us from the New World government official type people," he says.

"I like that," I tell him. "I hope I don't have to go jumping on rooftops in order to be one of you guys."

Aiden laughs, and I laugh with him. "No, nothing like that."

"Good," I tell him. I am used to heights and all from climbing trees, but I would not want to go jumping off of anything.

"You just have to kiss me," he says.

The both of us stop laughing and stare at each other.

It takes me a second to realize he's not serious, but I don't know if he wants me to actually kiss him or not. Is this a trick or some kind of joke? I mean, he's good looking and all, but I just met him, and kissing a stranger in a place where so many people have died just doesn't seem right. So why do I want to?

He leans in closer. "Relax, I'm joking," he says. I try to read his facial expression, but he looks away to stand up. He reaches out a hand for me, "Come on, we need to get back before the sun comes up."

CHAPTER 30

I take his hand and stand back up. Aiden looks over the edge of the tent and then lets go of my hand to make his way over to the first tree. When he moves to the second one, I move to the first. We continue this pattern until we are right back where we were at the Go Fishing game.

It's unfortunate that we have to come back here. The guards will know to look for us behind the game booths, but since there was no way out behind the main tent, the back of the booths is our only option.

We walk past the rock climbing wall and hide behind the next game booth on the other side of it. Aiden and I are moving slower than usual. I don't know about him, but my legs feel like they are about to fall off. I think sitting down for a few minutes was a bad idea since my legs somehow hurt more now than they did before.

When we get to the next game booth, there are more wires behind it than most of the others, so I am extra careful to make sure that I don't end up like Ethen. I can't help but wonder where

Ethen is now. I feel bad for leaving him there, but in a way, he did that to himself.

I think about what happened in his life to make him the way he is. How could someone grow up to wish their own brother dead? Was it his parent's fault, or was it his own?

He says that he worked at the library, but I don't remember ever seeing him in there, and I would go often. Did I ever say or do something to him to make him feel like he was less of a person?

I need to stop thinking about Ethen. I have to get out of here and back to Devin. I can't do that if I am thinking about other people.

We make our way back to the maze using our original method of moving behind the game booths and occasionally going inside the game booths. There are definitely more guards around, and it has gotten significantly darker.

Now that most of the game booths have been turned off, it has become harder to see where we are going and what we are stepping on. I try to move my feet around on the ground before I take a step in order to make sure I am not about to step on anything or get my foot caught on something. One wrong move and I could step on a twig, a guard could hear it, and we will be running around this place all over again. This can't happen because I am too tired of running. I simply just don't have the energy for it anymore.

When we get behind the next game booth, I move my feet slowly in order to not trip over any of the wires. This is difficult since some wires are sticking out in weird directions, and some of them have formed loops that my feet can easily get stuck in, so I try to be as careful as possible.

We cross over to the next booth and wait a minute. Aiden looks over the side of the booth and quickly puts his head back in the booth. I can just make out the shape of Aiden's face, and I know that it's not good. Someone must be coming.

About ten seconds later, I hear the footsteps, they are near us, but it sounds like it is just one guard. I look in the direction we came from, and I can see the faint outline of a person reflected on the booth we were previously behind. I tap my fingers on Aiden's hand to get his attention. When he looks at me, I point to the booth.

I know he understands this because he holds my hand tighter and inches closer to the edge of the booth, farther away from where the guard is heading. When the guard gets closer to the booth, and I can see the start of his foot coming our way, Aiden quickly moves to the front of the booth, and I do the same.

Once I am standing in front of the booth, I notice that the guard is just looking behind the game and not actually going entirely behind it. I can see the guards back towards us, and when he looks like he is about to come back to the front of the booth, Aiden and I rush to move back behind it.

My heart is racing, and it feels like we are running again, although we are not. The back of the booth is empty once more, with the exception of the wires. We wait behind the booth for the guard to leave. Aiden looks to the left while I look to the right in order to make sure the guard isn't going to look back here again.

When the sound of the guard's footsteps fades away, Aiden finally loosens his grip on my hand. This is not going to be easy. There are going to be more guards looking for us, and this time, they know where we like to hide.

I contemplate the idea of just running to the Mirror Maze and out of the carnival, but I know that it won't work out well. There is no way of outrunning the guards. Even if we make it to the maze without getting caught, we would still be leading the guards to everyone who is hiding in the woods.

I take a moment to close my eyes, take a deep breath in and exhale. When I am ready I look at Aiden and nod to let him know we can go.

We keep moving at a slow and tedious pace since we constantly have to stop and wait for one or more guards to pass. Most of the time, they just check the inside of the game booth, but other times, Aiden and I have to move around the booth since the guards will try to find us behind it. This means that we have to keep stopping, listening, and predicting what the guard's next move will be.

One time, a guard didn't just look behind the game booths, but instead, he circled the whole thing. Aiden and I did not know he was going to do this, and we nearly got caught while trying to move to the opposite side of the booth, away from the guard's eyesight. Each time we do this, I think we are going to get caught. I tell myself to prepare to try and fight the guard or run from him. Each time we don't get caught, I am a little bit relieved, but I know that it is going to happen again.

We move past two more game booths before having to cross a small opening over to another set of booths. The opening is small and poorly lit up due to the majority of the games no longer emitting a million bright lights. Once we are on the other side, there are about five more games we have to get through until we have to cross over again to another group of games, and then we will be at the maze.

We make it to the second game booth in this area when the sound of gunshots being fired is heard. The initial sound of the first shot being fired scares me, and I immediately believe we are being shot at, so I duck down as far as I can behind the booth. I cover my ears as the second and third shot is fired. I close my eyes as hard as I can since I know that at any second, one of these bullets are going to hit us.

I wait to feel some sort of pain, but nothing happens.

I feel Aiden crouch down beside me, "They are not shooting at us." Aiden says quietly next to my ear. "They are not shooting at us, Sam. The sound is coming from over by the main tent. They aren't near us. You are fine, we are okay. It's okay, Sam."

It takes me a minute to process the words he is saying. One more gunshot goes off, and I realize Aiden is right. The sound is coming from farther away and not from where we are.

I slowly open my eyes and see Aiden staring at me with a worried expression. It isn't until I take my hands away from my ears that I notice that I am crying. I don't know when I started crying, but it must have been at least a minute ago since my face is very wet.

"It's okay, Sam," Aiden says again.

He pulls me closer to him and gives me a sideways hug.

He tries to bring me to my feet, and once he does, he starts leading me inside the game booth. "Here, let's take a minute and hide in here," He says.

I recognize the game, it is the one with the horses on the table, and they are all lined up as if they are about to race. We had to get our horse to the finish line first in order to win. I try to remember the name of the game. Was it Race Track, Race Horse, or Race Me? I can't remember. It was definitely Race something.

Aiden and I go and hid under the table that has the horses on it. There is a small tarp that goes over the table and reaches about midway before the ground. We move to the back of it to make sure no one can see us if they were to look inside.

I sit there on the ground and bring my knees up to my chest. Aiden and I sit there for a few minutes in silence while I try to calm myself down. I try not to think about who the guards were shooting at, but I can't help it. These are innocent people. We all are. We don't deserve to be shot at or chased down.

The shooting came from over by the main tent. Does that mean that someone was trying to break out, or does it mean that they saw someone running around similar to me and Aiden? Was it Ethen they were shooting at, did he try to run from them?

I hate all of these questions in my head. They should not be there.

CHAPTER 31

The voices in my head are getting too loud, and they are not helping me calm down.

"Can you talk to me again? I think that helps," I tell Aiden when it starts becoming hard for me to breathe.

It takes a second for Aiden to start talking, "I was fifteen when I met Theon. We became friends almost instantly," Aiden lets out a little laugh. "I remember sitting at lunch one day in school, and all of a sudden, I got hit in the face with an apple. It hit me so hard it broke my jaw."

Aiden stops talking as the sound of footsteps approaches. He continues again after the sound fades. "He did not mean to hit me in the face, nonetheless, break my jaw, but he was fooling around with some of his friends, and I got caught in the crossfire. He kept apologizing to me long after I had forgiven him and told him to stop saying sorry. After that, though, we became best friends and hung out almost every day together."

"He didn't grow any less stupid as we got older," Aiden continues, "When we were seventeen, he tried to steal a bag of blueberries from our local store just to see if he could get away with it. He didn't. He thought that he could hide it in his pocket and no one would ask questions, but the blueberries stuck out, and the salesperson looked at him as if she knew, which she did, of course, since it was very obvious. Theon panicked and tried making a run for it. The second he ran out the door, he slipped on black ice, and he was caught instantly."

I try to picture it in my head as he is telling me this story, and the more I think about it, the funnier it is becoming.

"Wait, it gets better. I helped him up, and the salesperson told him that if he gave back what he had taken, then she wouldn't get him in trouble. When Theon went to take the berries out of his pocket, they were mostly smushed, and I guess Theon didn't know what to do at that point, so he scraped up as much of the berries as he could out of his pocket and handed it to the salesperson who looked at him with the most disgusted and shocked face. I swear it was one of the funniest things I have ever seen him do."

I have to fight to muffle the sound of my laughing. When I can catch my breath again, I ask him what happened next.

"So because Theon technically gave them back the blueberries, they had to let him go, so we left afterward, but each time we went into that same store after that, one of the salespeople had to follow him around. Luckily, he did it at one of the stores at the other end of town, so we didn't really need to visit it frequently unless it had something that the other stores didn't have, like salt," Aiden says.

"I don't understand it, but salt was so hard to get. Do you guys have that problem here?" Aiden asks.

"No, I never had trouble getting salt. It must be a Tundris thing," I tell him. "We have a problem getting things like fruit, but at least we can grow our own here when the weather is right."

Aiden turns his body more to face me better before speaking again. "We had a fruit problem, too, but it was always too cold to grow our own. We could grow apples, cherries, and peaches, though, which was nice, but that was about it."

"We did always have an abundance of acorns, though, so if you ever need those, then I know where to go. They were always around. If they were not falling on your head, then you were probably slipping on them," Aiden says.

I laugh at that, "What do you do with all of them?"

Aiden thinks for a second before responding. "Well, we had some people go around gathering them, and they would be turned into things like flour, or some people would bake and eat them or use them in decorations."

"Well, at least you were able to turn them into something instead of getting beaten up by acorns all day. Too bad you couldn't use them against the guards when they came."

"Yeah," Aiden says. We sit for another minute in silence, not saying or doing anything. I think the both of us are just tired. There is nothing left to say or do besides getting out of here.

Aiden is the first to speak again, "I am going to make them pay." The seriousness in his voice lets me know how committed he is to what he is saying. "I am going to get back at them. I don't know how, I don't know when, but I will. They can't get away with doing this with no punishment. I never expected this, any of this, no one did. I wish I knew sooner."

"It is not your fault." I tell him, "And you won't be getting back at them alone. You are not doing anything without me."

Aiden has his head down, and he doesn't seem to think much of what I just said, but I hope he knows how much I mean those words because I mean them with everything in me. It is not his fault. He didn't ask for any of this, he didn't cause this to happen. It was all our governors. He won't be doing anything alone, he has me, and I am sure he has the Jumpers on his side. I don't know how we are going to do it, but I know that we will. They will pay.

"We are going to get out of here. We are going to go from town to town, and we are going to warn people about what the New World government is doing." Aiden lifts his head to look at me as I speak, "We are going to stop the carnival from happening anywhere else, and we are going to prevent more people from dying. I promise that." I tell him.

"Okay then," Aiden says while he moves to stand back up. "I guess we should complete step one, getting out of here."

The story of Aiden and Theon calmed me down, and I am ready to get out of here. I don't think I will ever fully get rid of the immense amount of fear that built itself a home in my head since the government announced their "solution."

We stand up and make our way to the edge of the game booth and look to see if any guards are around. I can see the outline of a guard walking away in the distance, so I inch myself further into the booth and keep an eye on him.

Once the guard disappears from my sight, I check to make sure no one else is coming before making my way behind the next game booth. Like the booth we were just in, this one has its lights turned off. Unlike the booth we were just in, this one has a lot more wires around it, and I have to be extra careful not to trip and fall. This is a whole lot easier said than done since it is very dark and almost pitch black behind the booth.

I try putting my arms out to hold onto the tarp covered fence and the back of the game booth, but the sound the fence makes is too loud for my liking, and I put both arms on the booth. I shuffle my feet around and try to make small steps, so I do not end up getting tangled in the wires. When I make it about halfway behind the booth, Aiden joins me.

He seems to be having just as hard a time as me because he is moving slowly as well. When I make it to the edge of the booth, I look out at the area around us once more. When I do, I can immediately tell that something happened.

The lights that were on just minutes ago are now off. The lights that made it possible for me to see the guards before are now nowhere to be found.

My heart skips a beat at this, but I push down the panic that I am feeling inside. It's okay. It's all going to be okay. If you can't see them, then they can't see you.

I jump a little when Aiden lightly taps me on the shoulder. I look back at him, and then I quickly turn to look at the other side of the game booth again. It is still pitch black, and I can't tell if anyone is around. I turn back to Aiden, whose face I can just make out in the dark.

"It is dark. Very, very dark. I can't see anything," I tell Aiden in as quiet of a whisper as I can. "I can't tell if there are any guards around."

Aiden moves in front of me while keeping one hand on the booth for what I assume is for stability and looks out from behind the booth to see for himself. When he is done looking, he turns back towards me with a slightly concerned look, but it goes away almost instantly.

"We will just have to move slower and quieter," he whispers to me with his face so close to mine. I nod my head in understanding, and he looks at me for another second before moving to the next game booth. I wait until he sounds far enough away for me to join him.

I move slowly and cautiously over to the next game booth. I try to make the transition from one booth to the other quickly since the last thing I need is some guard turning on a flashlight, and I end up getting spotted instantly.

After two more booths, Aiden stops, and I almost walk right into his back. He turns around, and I can see by the look on his face someone must be coming. Aiden points to his ear, so I listen to see if I can hear anything. It only takes me a few seconds before I hear the footsteps that Aiden must have heard.

I motion my head for Aiden to peek out of the booth on the side closest to him, and I will look out the booth on the side closer to me. The footsteps sound far away enough that I think it is safe to check. I want to know how the guards plan on finding us. I don't see the reflection of light coming from anywhere, so I don't think they are using flashlights, but if they are not using flashlights, then how would they see us? Have they given up?

I bet they haven't. This is probably just a new strategy.

I make my way over to the side of the booth opposite from Aiden, and I slowly move my head to look at the other side. Like before, the other side is pitch black, and I can only see the outline of a few things. I can barely make out the game booth I see across the way, but I am pretty sure that it is one of the booths we used when we were crossing over from the kitchen the second time. If I am right, then it is almost a straightaway walk to the Mirror Maze.

I keep looking around the area, trying to spot where the guard went, but I can't. I wince, and my heart abruptly starts racing when I feel a hand on my shoulder. I calm down when I look to see that it is just Aiden's hand. I think that is the second time now he has nearly given me a heart attack.

Aiden moves behind me and leans over my shoulder. "Over there, look a little left of the tree," Aiden says.

I look to see where he is pointing, but I do not spot a person. There is only a tiny green light. I stare at it, trying to find out why Aiden would want me to look at it.

"What about it?" I ask Aiden after another minute goes by, and nothing has happened.

"Keep looking," is all Aiden says.

It only takes about ten seconds after Aiden speaks for me to see what he is talking about. The green light starts to move around slowly. No, it is not just moving around, it is attached to something.

I keep my eyes on it and try to see if there is a pattern or cause for the light being there. When I can't figure it out, I move back fully behind the game booth and turn my body to face Aiden.

"What is that?" I ask him.

"I don't know. I have never seen them use anything like that before."

I think for another second before asking another question, "Do you think it is dangerous? Do you think they can see us with that?"

"I don't know. I would not put it past them to use some sort of technology to hunt us down. I think we will be fine if we continue the way we have been, but we just have to be extra careful and avoid whatever it is."

I agree. I don't know what that moving light means, but I really do not want to find out. We are not far from the Mirror Maze now, and we can't risk getting caught and having to run around the whole carnival again.

Chapter 32

Aiden moves back to the edge of the booth, looks out at the other side, and after a few seconds, he makes his way to the next booth. I do the same as him and look around at the other side of the booth before I cross to the next game. I no longer see the green light, and I don't hear any footsteps, so I take that as a good sign and make my way over to where Aiden is.

We cross to the next booth, then the next. I can see tables when I look around the side of the booth, which lets me know we are around the food court area.

As I am about to cross to the next booth, I notice the green light has appeared again. This one is closer to us, only about a hundred feet away to our right. As it gets closer, I am able to get a better look at it, and the longer I stare, I realize that it is not just a light but part of a helmet.

The green light is coming from a visor on the top of a helmet that a guard is wearing. I immediately get back behind the booth and hope the guard didn't see me. I don't know for sure, but I think the helmet helps them see in the dark.

Fear rushes through my body again, and I try to spot Aiden, who is at the back of the booth right next to me. I can just see the outline of him, but I know he is probably wondering what I am doing. I point my finger in the direction of the guard, hoping that Aiden can see it and understand what I am trying to say.

I can hear the guard's footsteps coming closer, and I don't know what to do. They know we like to hide behind the games, they will look here. Without thinking, I duck down low and walk into the game booth that Aiden is hiding behind. From this angle, I don't think the guard can see me, but he definitely will if I am right, and he walks over here in a few seconds.

Aiden follows me in, staying low to the ground like I did. I can see the confusion on his face, but I don't have time to explain. I know we are in a food booth, and they have cabinets and drawers, so I head over to the larger cabinets at the front of the booth and open them.

There are a few paper plates and napkins on one side of it and a few bottles of condiments on the other side. I point at the other cabinet for Aiden, and I think he seems to get what I am trying to say. He quickly opens his and starts to get inside. Once he does though, he immediately turns back and quietly starts slowly opening some of the larger drawers on the counter next to us.

I am confused at first, but then I realize he has a bigger and longer gun. Therefore, it won't fit in the cabinet with him, and he has to hide it somewhere else.

He finds one big enough for his gun quickly, and then he comes back to the cabinets. He gets into his, and I get into mine, but I have to ensure I don't knock over any of the bottles. I sit on top of the paper plates and napkins and hover my feet above the bottles.

I hear the guard's steps get closer. He must be only about five steps away from us. I close the cabinet door as quietly as I can and wait to hear the sound of anything happening.

It is like I am hyper-aware of everything. I can hear the sound of feet as they walk by the cabinet I am sitting in, and I can tell that there is more than one guard now. I hear the sound of shuffling going on around us, but I don't think it is all coming from inside the booth we are in. I think they sent a group to this area to check the booths over here.

When the sound of the guards becomes faint and less frequent, I relax a little bit. My legs are starting to get tired from hovering over the bottles, but I do not let them fall. The last thing I need is to make one of the bottles fall over and alert all the guards that I am inside here.

I stay in the cabinet longer in order to make sure all of the guards have left. I close my eyes for a moment, and I have trouble reopening them. I realize now that I am exhausted, and I want to go to bed. Who knows how long I have been up for.

There is a quiet tap on the door, and then I hear it open. My eyes open back up right away, and I look over to see that it is Aiden.

"What, are you sleeping in here or something? The guards are gone, and we need to go." As Aiden is saying this, I start to make my way out of the cabinet, and I give him a slight glare.

"Don't look at me like that. You can sleep once we make it out of here," Aiden says.

I stand up, and the two of us look around the area before heading over to the drawer where Aiden put his gun. When he opens it, his gun is still inside. He grabs it, and we head back behind the booths.

"So I take it you saw all the guards coming our way," Aiden says.

"No. I only saw the one. He was wearing a helmet with a green visor. I think that was the green light we saw earlier. I guessed that they could probably see us with it, so I figured we needed to hide somewhere they would be less likely to look."

Aiden thinks about this for a second, "good thinking," he says and then continues walking behind the game booths.

We make it pretty far, and we are only about three or four booths away from the maze. We move slowly, but we are moving without any trouble. Neither of us has tripped or gotten caught on a wire, and there have not been any more groups of guards walking around. There is the occasional single guard and sometimes two guards walking together, but ultimately, they are far enough away or looking somewhere else, so we don't have to worry too much about them.

We cross to the back of the next booth and then the next booth after that. I can see the opening up ahead that leads to where the maze is, and I can't help but get a little excited. After all of that running around, we can finally get out of here, and I can see Devin again.

When we reach the end of the booth, Aiden takes a look at the other side to make sure no one is coming before he crosses to the next booth. Usually, when there is no one coming, he crosses over quickly. Since he does not do that this time, I know that there must be one or more guards around.

Aiden turns back at me and puts one finger up. I do not know if this means there is one guard or if we need to wait one minute before crossing. When the sound of faint footsteps are heard, I know that it is the first one.

I put my back against the back of the booth and look to the right while Aiden looks to the left. By doing this, we are making sure at least one of us can spot the guard if he decides to come back here.

I hear the sound of a struggle coming from my left, and I immediately whip my head around to look at Aiden. I see he has his hand over the guard's mouth, but the guard is pushing him away with one hand and reaching for something on his waistband with the other. When I notice the guard is trying to grab his gun, I move to push his arm out of the way of it and grab the gun myself.

This fails, and I end up having to use both arms to pull his hand away from his gun. In one quick motion, Aiden moves around so that his body is behind the guard's. He takes his hand off the guard's mouth, wraps one arm around the guard's neck, and puts the other on his head. The guard stops fighting me and instead tries to grab at Aiden's arm. When this does not work, he then tries to move forward and backward to shake Aiden off.

I don't know what to do, so I take the guard's gun out of his holster and point it at him just in case he manages to get free. Then I just stand there watching, feeling useless. Aiden looks like he has the guard relatively under control, so I look around to make sure there aren't any more green lights. When I am sure No one else is coming, I look back at Aiden, who has a good hold of the guard.

The guard is still trying to fight him, but his movements are slower now and less effective. Within a few seconds, the guard's eyes close, and he passes out. Aiden slowly drops the guard's body down to the ground.

"Are you okay?" I ask Aiden.

"Yeah. Are you okay?" Aiden asks, and I nod my head to let him know I am alright.

Aiden's shoulders rise and fall with each breath he takes, and I know that fighting the guard must have tired him out.

I don't know why I do it, but I walk up to Aiden and kiss him. He is taken aback by this, so I start to pull away. When I do, his hand comes up to my face, and he deepens the kiss.

After a minute, I pull away. While I do like kissing Aiden, I don't know him or why I did it. Besides, I do not think right now is the time to be kissing anybody.

He grabs my hand and starts pulling me behind the last game booth. "Come on, we need to go. He won't be out for long."

It is a good thing he does not want to talk about it. If he asked why I kissed him, I don't think I would have been able to give him an answer.

"Wait," I tell him

"Sam, we need to go. Once he wakes up, he will let everyone know where we are and what direction we are headed in."

I free my hand from his and bend down to grab the guard's helmet. "Now we can go," I tell him as I push the helmet into his hands. "You can put that on. We will be quicker if one of us can see."

"Why don't you want it?" Aiden asks.

"Because you are the leader here, and besides, you just took the guard out, so you should get the helmet." I tuck the little gun that the guard had in one of my jacket pockets, "Besides, I now have two guns, so you have to do what I say, and I say put the helmet on and lead us out of here."

Aiden mumbles a fine and puts the helmet on.

"Can you see?" I ask.

"Yes, it is a little cracked on the bottom, but it works." Aiden retakes my hand, "Let's go."

Chapter 33

It does not take us long to reach the Mirror Maze. We make it there within five minutes or so. We make our way to the exit of the maze and enter.

The previous times we were in here, I had to let my eyes adjust to the blinding bright lights that made out the outline of the mirrors. This time that does not happen. The guards must have turned off the power to the building or just turned off the lights in general. Either way, it is pitch black in there.

Aiden gives my hand a squeeze. "Don't let go of my hand."

Aiden walks in first since he has the helmet on, the perks of being able to see in the dark. I follow him inside and close the door behind me. The second I do this, I become very aware that I can't see anything aside from the green light on Aiden's helmet. If it were not for that light, then I would have thought that I had gone blind.

Aiden walks slowly, and I try to do my best not to walk into him. I use my free hand to feel for any mirrors and decoys to avoid walking into them.

"What's wrong?" I whisper to Aiden when he stops walking.

"I used the lights along the borders of the mirrors to see where to go last time. The door to the outside is on a mirror with a slightly larger border of light around it. Now that the lights have been turned off, I am having a hard time figuring out where to go."

"I guess we will just guess then. I mean, we have the time, right? The sun won't be rising for at least another hour or two. We will just have to keep a listen to hear if anyone comes in here," I tell him.

"Okay, let's try this way first, then."

Aiden leads my hand to the left, and we continue that way for a while before he stops abruptly, and I walk right into him. He puts his hand on my waist to help stabilize me after I lose my balance.

"Sorry," he says. "I think I just walked us into a corner."

The light hearted way he just said that makes me want to laugh. I fight it, though, since right now doesn't feel like the right time to be laughing at anything. I take a few steps back so Aiden can get around me, and when he does, he starts leading the both of us through the maze again.

The singular green light from Aiden's helmet reflects on the mirror around us. Walking around here with him feels like stepping inside a kaleidoscope. If he weren't holding my hand, then I would have no idea where he actually was. Sometimes, I can see the reflection of the light off in the distance. Other times, it looks like he is standing to the left and right of me all at the same time.

We continue to make a few more turns, and then Aiden stops again. He lets out a frustrated sigh and states, "We are back at the start of the maze. We are going to have to do this all over again."

I move to the side to let Aiden pass me, and I try to come up with ways to get us out of here faster so that we won't end up stuck in this maze all night.

"Why don't we try pushing on the mirrors a little bit? Maybe we will end up opening the door out of dumb luck," I suggest.

"We can try that, but I am afraid of knocking a mirror down and drawing attention to ourselves."

"We can still try it, but we just have to be careful not to push too hard," I tell him.

Aiden says okay, and as we make our way through the maze again, I give light pushes on the mirrors and probably the decoys, too. I can't tell the difference.

The ones that wobble let me know that they are placed in an area with no wall behind it, and therefore, I am pushing on stuff that is unstable and could crash down, so I push lighter. Once I push on something and it does not wobble, I know a wall is behind it, and we are getting closer to where the door is.

We take a few more turns and get caught in three more corners, but we keep moving on. We make another turn just as I hear the sound of a door closing. I look at Aiden, and I can tell from the green light reflecting on his face that he heard it, too.

The two of us start frantically pushing on the mirrors, trying to find where the door is. The mirrors start getting wobbly again, and I do not think we missed the door. We are probably at the wrong wall.

Aiden starts pulling my hand around the maze faster. I do not know if the guard knows we are in here or if he is just doing a general check, but I really do not want him to find us.

We are relatively quiet as we move through the maze, and I try to look around to see if I see anything. I assume the guard has a helmet on like the others, so I try to look for the green light that comes from it, but I don't think I will be able to spot the difference between the guard's light and Aiden's.

All I see is various sizes of green lights reflecting from all around, and it is stressing me out. Are these all Aidens, or is it from another guard? How many guards came in here?

Honestly, we only heard the sound of a door closing, a guard could have only peaked his head in and then left, or there could have already been one in here before we were, and they just left. I doubt that last thought since we have been in here forever and have circled this place at last twice. I try to tell myself that the first option is the truth and that we will be alright.

I try lightly pushing on the mirrors and decoys as we pass by them, but nothing is sturdy. I almost want to push them all to the floor to find the door, but that would not only give away our location by attracting guards to the sound. It would probably also break the mirrors, and we would have to watch where we step to ensure we don't cut ourselves. It's just a bad idea.

Aiden stops instantly, and I walk into him once again. He still holds my hand, but he uses his other one to wrap around my shoulders and led us back to wherever we just came from.

As Aiden is rushing us back in that direction, he whispers in my ear, "I saw the guard. I think it is only the one."

I think about trying to hide from the guard. If there is only one, then maybe we can hide long enough for him to walk through the maze and leave. The only problem with this plan is that there is no good place to hide in here. We could try hiding ourselves in a corner and hope the guard doesn't find us there, but that is unlikely, and if we do end up getting spotted, then we would have nowhere to run.

I let Aiden lead us wherever since he is the one who can see. We keep moving. Aiden abruptly turns around sometimes to head back where we came, and I can only assume it is because he saw the guard. I realize now that all of these mirrors and decoys might be confusing when seeing other people in the maze. Is Aiden actually seeing the guard, or is he seeing a reflection of himself?

We turn a corner, and I spot the guard only a few feet away. I can tell this is not Aiden since the guard's green light from his helmet is higher up by about three or four inches. The guard is facing our direction, and I just know in my gut that he has seen us.

Aiden quickly turns back around, and we start moving in the opposite direction again. I can't help feeling like we have been running back and forth through this maze at least ten times.

We make another turn, and the guard is right there. Aiden tries to turn us around to run, but the guard punches him in the face, and he falls. I feel the guard's hand grab my upper arm, and I try to pull away. He doesn't release me, and his grip doesn't loosen at all, so I try to kick at him. This is hard to do since the only thing I can see is the light from his helmet.

I kick what I believe to be his knee, and he lets go of my left arm. I use this opportunity to try and grab the gun that is in the waistband of my jeans. As soon as I have it in my hands, the guard smacks my forearms hard, and the gun falls to the floor. He then punches me in the face, and the next thing I know, I am on the ground.

Pain. That is all I feel at first. Then, there is a throbbing sensation that comes next. I touch the side of my head where he punched me, but it stings. I don't think it is bleeding, so that is good. At least, I think it's a good thing. I'm not a doctor, so I don't know. I am going to hope it's good, though.

I think I see Aiden get up, but it is hard to tell. I feel around the ground, trying to find where the gun went, when I remember that I have a second one in my pocket from the guard Aiden knocked out before we came here.

I raise the gun, but I have no idea where to point it. I can't tell who is who anymore with the both of them fighting. I can see their heads moving around, and I can hear the sound of fists connecting with something on someone's body, but I can't actually see their bodies or what exactly is going on. I don't want to shoot and accidentally kill Aiden.

"Aiden, flashlight!" I yell, hoping he will have a chance to give me the flashlight he took from one of the guards in the kitchen.

I don't know what happens next, but both of them fall, taking a few mirrors down with them from the sound of it. I wince at the sound of glass shattering, and I hope Aiden is alright.

Another second goes by before I hear the two of them fighting again. I try feeling on the ground for anything, and my hand eventually lands on what feels like a metal object. I feel around some more, and I realize that it is the flashlight. I do not know if Aiden threw it to me or if it just fell out of his pocket, but I quickly turn it on to get a better look at what is going on.

I wave the flashlight around until I can see that Aiden and the guard are now standing up. Aiden no longer has his helmet on, and the guard takes another swing at his head. Aiden dodges it and backs up a little from the guard. I can see blood on both of them, and it looks like the side of Aiden's face must be cut because there is a stream of blood running down his face and neck. His gun is no longer in sight, but it doesn't look like the guard has his gun on him either, so this makes me feel better.

"I thought I saw Governor Wood's son walking around here earlier. Long time no see," the guard says, looking at Aiden. When he sees me pointing the gun at him, he puts his hands up and doesn't move.

I take a look at Aiden's face to see if he knows what the guard is talking about, but Aiden just looks angry and ready to fight the guard some more. I point my gun at the guard and get ready to warn him that I will shoot him if he moves.

"You two are really working together? Now, I would not have expected that. Does your father know where you are, Atlas?" The guard says.

I stop thinking about warning the guard about shooting him, and I instead decide I want to know what he is talking about. "What do you mean?"

"You didn't tell her?" The guard says in a taunting tone.

"Sam-"

Aiden's words get cut off by the guard, "Atlas, here is the son of Governor Alfred Wood," he says to me. The guard then turns back to Aiden, "You know there have been a lot of people looking for you. Most people thought you died."

I look at Aiden in disbelief and wait for him to say something, but he doesn't. "Aiden?" I say, trying to get him to explain.

"Aiden? Is that the name you go by now? Interesting." The guard says the last word with a hint of ridicule.

I look at Aiden again," Aiden! Is it true!"

The guard takes this moment to lunge at me and knock the gun out of my hand again. He punches me and then pushes me into what I assume is a mirror. I fall through, shattering it in the process. Pain races from my shoulder and down my arm.

I hear Aiden yell something that I can't make out the words to. I reach around on the ground, trying to feel for the flashlight I dropped at some point in my fall. When I finally find it, I look up and shine it around the room. I can see the guard standing a few feet from me, and I see Aiden run at the guard and tackle him down.

At first, Aiden is on top of him, punching the guard, but then the guard manages to flip them over so that Aiden is on his back. The guard puts his hands around Aiden's neck and starts choking him.

I search around the ground, trying to find either one of the guns I had, but I can't seem to find one. I know I don't have much time, so I pick up the biggest shard of glass I can see and quickly run to Aiden. I stab the glass into the guard's shoulder with as much strength as I can. The guard yells in pain, looks at his shoulder, and then looks at me.

I see the look of anger in his eyes as he lets go of Aiden, grabs my neck, and throws me down to the ground. He leans over me with his hand still on my neck. I struggle to grab at his hands to get them off of me, and when that doesn't work, I kick my feet up, but it is no use. The guard is too strong. It is becoming harder and harder to breathe as he applies more pressure.

There is a loud bang, and the pressure on my neck disappears. I start to be able to breathe again as the guard's grip on my neck weakens, and I see the guard's body fall to the ground. I crawl away from the guard and over to Aiden. I see Aiden holding his gun up, and the look of fear and terror is written on his face.

I point the flashlight back over to the guard, and I can see blood coming out of the side of his head. Aiden killed him.

"Aiden..." My voice comes out barely audible.

"We need to go now," Aiden says, still in shock, "The guards will have heard that, and they will all be coming here."

I wave my flashlight on the ground until I find both the guns I dropped. I pick them up, and when I turn back to look for Aiden, I see he has found the door. I guess it is easy to find the door when most of the mirrors have been knocked down. He has his gun in one hand and one of the helmets in the other. I walk over to him and turn the flashlight off.

Aiden does not say anything. He just simply opens the door and walks out.

CHAPTER 34

I close the door behind me as I exit the maze. By the time I turn around, Aiden is already halfway across to the tree line. I run to catch up, and I reach him right as he is just entering the woods.

It is still dark out, but the sky is slowly starting to brighten. The sun must be coming up in an hour or so.

"Aiden, slow down," I tell him. "We need to talk!"

"Talk about what?" He says, sounding frustrated. "Talk about who my father is or talk about how I just killed someone?"

I don't even know what to say. Both of those things aren't sitting right with me, and I know they aren't with Aiden either. At least, I don't think they are sitting right with him. Who knows? Maybe Aiden is faking the whole thing. After all, if what the guard said was true, then Aiden is Governor Wood's son—the same governor who played a part in killing innocent people tonight.

I don't know anything about any of the three governor's children, certainly not Governor Wood's, and as far as I am aware, no one does. If Aiden is the son of one of the governors who planned these deadly carnivals, then how could I trust him?

"Are you really his son?" I ask, although I am afraid to know the answer. I like Aiden. I have just spent who knows how long running around this dam carnival trying not to get killed with him, and he helped me. I want the answer to be no, but I don't think it is.

Aiden stops walking and looks at me with a quick, sad smile. "That would be me. Atlas Wood, son of Governor Alfred Wood."

He looks me in the eyes and waits for my response. I am once again at a loss for words, and I stand there opening and closing my mouth, struggling to say anything.

After another minute, I finally regain my composure. "Do the Jumpers know?" It sounds like a stupid question, but I am curious.

"Only a select few," Aiden says.

"How..." I don't even know what I am asking, but somehow Aiden does.

"I lived in the town of Officials for fourteen years, and I hated every second of it." The look of disgust drapes over Aiden's face. "My parents were not the best, but I thought everyone else was relatively alright since they didn't bother me too much. The town of officials is terrible. No one there cares about anyone. I was at my breaking point when I overheard my parents talking about sending me into the military once I turned fifteen since that is the minimum age requirement. They wanted me to go over the wall and fight to steal what others had."

"You mean in no man's land? There are people there?" I ask in surprise.

Aiden leans back against a tree. "No. I mean over the wall. The wall is beyond no man's land. It is the thing separating us from the people on the other side. No man's land isn't really that bad. Most of the bad things people hear about it are fake and made up so that people wouldn't want to go beyond the town walls. The government did it to get better control of the people living in the New World."

"I didn't want to fight the people beyond the wall. They already have so little, and it wouldn't be fair." Aiden continues, "The New World destroyed most of the Fritts in the war. Only about a hundred survived and were let go once they promised never to return. I have no idea where they went, but I know they were not all killed like the history books tell people. The people beyond the wall aren't the Fritts. They have no country. They are all simply just trying to survive with what little is left of the world."

I let all of that sink in.

The Fritts were never all killed? Some of them survived? The government lied to us? Of course they did. They have been lying to us about the carnival. Why wouldn't they lie about everything else? They have been lying from the start.

If what Aiden is saying is true, then there are other people out there beyond the wall. It is not just the New World anymore. They told us there were no other people or countries, but that might all be one big lie—or Aiden is lying.

"How do I know I can trust you? You could be lying to me."

"I know I don't deserve your trust because I kept it all a secret," Aiden says. "I guess all I can tell you is that I lived in Tundris for six years, and in that time, I became my own person and not the person my parents wanted me to be. I am not them."

"How did you get to Tundris?" I ask him. How on earth did he leave the town of Officials without anyone knowing? He is the son of one of the three governors. Eyes must have been all over him.

"I had the same bodyguard for three years. We got pretty close within that time. I told him what I heard about my parents wanting to put me in the military, and he told me he would help me escape if I wanted to." Aiden continues, "I said yes. Two months later, I finally got out, and he took me to Tundris under a fake name. He gave me a cover story and told everyone that my parents had died, and I was moved to a new town so I wouldn't have to be reminded of their deaths."

"Who took care of you then?"

"A man named Balan took me in. He was a police officer in Tundris, and he is back at the Jumpers camp right now. He is one of the ones who knows who I really am," Aiden says.

"So your real name is Atlas?" I ask just to clarify.

"Yes," Aiden says with a look of longing.

"Do you like that name better?"

"I like the name better, but I do not like who it ties me to," Aiden hangs his head low, and I can tell he blames himself for the things his father has done.

"If you left six years ago, then you had no idea about the New World's problems or what the governors were planning to do. Their actions are not your own," I tell Aiden, but he does not look like he believes me.

"If I had never left, then maybe I would have been there to hear their plans and suggested something better. Or maybe I could have waited and left after they came up with their plan, and I could have gotten out to warn people sooner." Aiden's eyes start to water, and I know that he feels guilty, although he did nothing wrong.

"You can't think about the what ifs. You have to think about the things you did do. You got us out of the carnival. You got me back in so I could look for my father. You got me back out." I slowly walk towards Aiden, but he just looks away from me. "And now, because of you, that group of people waiting in the woods back there are going to live."

"Because of me, that guard is dead," he says. A tear falls from his face, and as I get closer to him, I see that his whole body is shaking.

I close the gap between us and try to hug him. He pushes my arms away and tries to fight me off, but he eventually gives up and lets me wrap my arms around him. I just hold him, not saying anything and just letting him get it all out.

I don't know what kind of state I would be in if it had been me who killed the guard. As much as I would like to believe that I would not cry since the guard was willing to kill us, the reality is I would be like Aiden since I don't think I could ever take someone's life away from them.

When Aiden's body stops shaking, and I no longer hear his cries, I loosen up my hold on him.

"I have never killed anyone before..." Aiden says, his voice sounding broken. "I never wanted to hurt anyone."

"I know," I tell him, tightening my hold on him again.

"Why don't you hate me?" He asks.

The question throws me off guard.

Why don't I hate him? He is the son of one of the governors who did this to us. I should be mad, but I am not. "This wasn't your fault. None of it was. I hate your father and the other governors. I don't hate you."

After another minute, Aiden says, "They are going to be leaving soon. We should return to the others before they take off without us."

I release Aiden from my arms and start walking through the woods, trying to find where the group is.

"Didn't you grow up here?" Aiden asks.

"Of course I did. What about it?"

"I am just surprised, is all. I thought someone who grew up in these woods would know that they were going the wrong way."

I glare at Aiden and throw my hands up in frustration. "How do you know this place better than me?"

"I don't know. I guess I just have better directional skills than you," Aiden says. I can still hear a hint of sadness in his voice, but regardless of this, he is trying to lighten the mood. It just so happened that it involves picking on me.

"Don't tell my brother. I always make fun of him for not knowing where he is going."

We walk in silence for a little longer before I bring the mood back down. "Are you okay… physically?" I ask him.

"I am fine. It is just some cuts and bruises. I feel fine now, but it will probably hurt more in the morning. Are you okay?"

"Yeah, I am fine. I have some small cuts from the mirrors, but other than that, I am alright." My arm is still throbbing a little from when I fell, and I know it has been cut pretty badly by the glass as well, but I don't say anything because I know it's minor compared to Aiden. My throat hurts a little from when the guard tried choking me as well, but I don't mention that either. "And by the way, I think it is technically morning."

Aiden looks up at the sky which is getting brighter by the minute. It is not quite time for the sun to come up, but it is getting close. He smirks at my comment, and the two of us continue walking through the woods to the group.

"So does being the governor's son mean you won't kiss me anymore, or are you still open to that?" Aiden says in a playful tone as we get closer to where we are going.

My eyes widen, and I lightly smack the side of his arm, "Aiden!" I have to turn my head so he doesn't see me smile. "Why did you even let me kiss you in the first place?" I ask with a little laugh.

"Do you really think I would turn down a kiss from someone who looks like you? Besides, you practically attacked me," Aiden is now smiling, and I can't help but smile back.

I see the group in the distance, "I did not attack you. It was simply an in-the-moment thing."

After I say that, I rush towards the group and quickly find Devin.

Devin immediately brings me in for a big hug the second he sees me. I hug him back as hard as I can. How do I tell my brother that our father is dead? I went back into the carnival to find our Dad, but I came back empty handed.

"I didn't find him," I tell Devin. "I think they killed him," I say this last part so quietly I am surprised Devin even hears me.

"I know," Devin says. "But you came back. I still have my sister, and that is all that matters."

Devin lets go of me, and once he gets a better look at me, I can see his expression change from happy to worried. "Are you alright? What happened in there?" he asks.

"I can ask the same thing," Theon says.

Theon comes to stand next to my brother and Aiden. He is looking at Aiden and me with a lot of curiosity. He looks at the blood on Aiden's face, and then he looks over to me, where I have about twenty small cuts on my arms from the broken mirrors.

"It's a long story," I tell them. "I am alright, just minor things," I tell Devin.

"What? Did you go shopping while you were in there?" Theon says while eyeing up the guard jacket that I stole. I glare at him and want to say something in response, but Aiden speaks before I can.

"We need to get going. We cannot wait any longer," Aiden says. I will explain everything that happened on the way, but we need to go right now. It won't take long for the guards to figure out we left through the door in the Mirror Maze. Once they find that out, they will be heading this way. We need to be long gone by the time they do that."

"Okay, then, let's go," Theon says.

Aiden and Theon gather everyone up and start walking further into the woods, where there is a fence. The fence is part of what keeps us in Treegrass. We are not supposed to break it or try to get over it. At least, that is what we have been told.

Aiden and Theon both pick up the bottom of the chain-link fence and hold it open for people to crawl under it. People start crawling under the fence one by one, and I try to see if I recognize anyone.

There are a few faces of people I have seen around Treegrass, but no one that I actually know. I see the young girl I got out of the carnival with the first time, and I am happy to see that she looks comfortable with the people she is with.

I notice that I have not seen Vesper, the guy that Aiden was talking to when I interrupted him to talk him into bringing me back into the carnival. I wait until it is my turn to go under the fence before asking about him.

"He took some of the injured people back to our camp on the ATVs. Some of them were hurt really badly and needed medical help. We will have to walk there on foot, but I honestly think we would have had to do that anyway, given the amount of people," Theon says.

I crawl under the fence and feel like I am leaving home for the final time. I don't want to go, but I know I can't stay.

I have to move on.

Chapter 35

It feels like we have been walking for hours.

My feet hurt. My head hurts. My neck hurts. Everything hurts.

I do not say anything to anyone since I know I am not the only one hurting. Aiden and Theon keep saying that the Jumper camp is just a few more miles ahead, but it feels like we have walked halfway across the world.

Most of what we have walked through has been woods. Sometimes, we come across a stream or a road, but most of the time, all I see are trees, branches, bugs, and dirt.

I walk with Devin only a few feet behind Theon and Aiden. The rest of the group walks behind us, and I can't help but feel sorry for them. Every time I look back to see how they are doing, their lifeless eyes look back at me. They reminded me of the eyes of the dead people behind the show tent. No matter how hard I try, I can't seem to shake that memory. There were just so many.

"Are you ready to tell me what happened in there?" Theon asks.

"No. I want to wait until we are farther from Treegrass. I don't want any of the shooters to go searching for us and find us sitting on a tree trunk telling stories," Aiden says. "I want to put as much distance between us and them as possible."

We keep walking, and the thick forest full of tall trees eventually starts disappearing until all that is left are tree stumps—a whole lot of tree stumps. There is a clearing completely devoid of trees for what looks like miles. Just the bottoms of cut-down trees and tall grass are seen.

Aiden and Theon lead us across it, and I can't help but wonder what went on here. Who cut all these trees down, and why?

"What is all of this?" Devin asks.

Aiden answers, "I don't really know for sure, but someone at some point in time cut all the trees down. From what I can tell, this was a whole forest until the trees were taken away. The stumps don't look that rotted, so they were probably cut down within only ten years or so ago. My guess is that the New World did it, but honestly, who knows."

"Could it be anyone else?" I ask. We are in no man's land, and Aiden said another wall was blocking the outside world from us here, so it couldn't be anyone else, right?

"There have been stories of outsiders getting in and scavenging, but nothing has ever been confirmed," Theon states. "If the stories are true, then maybe some came in here and decided to steal the forest."

I doubt someone would come into the New World just to steal a few hundred, maybe a thousand, trees. How on earth would they carry them back? It had to be the New World's doing, but why?

I can't stop staring at it. All these stumps everywhere make me want to cry. It feels like someone tried destroying my own home. I can't imagine all the trees in Treegrass ever getting cut down, they show our history, and they are part of who we are.

I almost trip several times because I am too busy looking around the open area rather than looking at where I am stepping. I can see more trees in the distance to the left, but they are far, and only a few of them exist.

It takes us about forty-five more minutes of walking before I can see trees up close again. The tall oak trees look like a wall bordering all the cut-down trees. It is as if the people who cut them down decided to draw a line, and all the trees on one side got cut down while the others got to remain.

When we walk into the woods, I quickly realize that the terrain is different here than in Treegrass. The woods here are denser and more challenging to walk through.

"Watch your step!" Theon yells to the group.

Aiden looks back at the group calmly and says, "There is a road up ahead, so the walk will get easier. Our camp is not much further now, maybe about an hour or so."

"It would have been nice if they had brought the ATVs back after they dropped the injured off," I hear Theon mumble.

I try not to think about the pain in my feet, and instead, I try to focus on where we are heading. I do not look back or around at our surroundings. I just focus on what is ahead of me and where my feet are going.

About another half an hour passes when Theon speaks again. "So, do you think we are far enough that you are ready to talk about what happened to you guys in the carnival?" He asks while glancing at Aiden and me.

I look at Aiden, and he looks back at me. Neither of us are ready to talk about it, but I know that Theon is dying to know.

"We found the room relatively easy," I say. "Everything else was a little bit harder."

"I bet. You guys were in there for probably about five hours at least," Theon says. "I had to practically tackle this one down," Theon points to Devin, "to stop him from trying to go in himself."

I look at Devin, and he looks unapologetically back at me. I can't blame him. If the roles were reversed, I would have been the same way.

"Sam got the list along with a map," Aiden says, "while I distracted them from the room. We met back up in the kitchen... then we tried to make our way back to the maze, but there were guards everywhere." I notice that Aiden doesn't mention Ethen, and I understand why. He tried to save Ethen, but Ethen got caught, and we had to leave him behind. While it might have been Ethan's fault for getting caught, I can tell that Aiden still blames himself for it.

"A lot happened. Let's just say it was good that we got out of there when we did. Who knows what they would have come up with next if we stayed. The shooters were getting clever in there and turned all the lights off so we couldn't see. They used these helmets," Aiden says and holds up the helmet in his hand to show Theon, "to see in the dark. We got one off of a guard and used it ourselves. When we were leaving through the maze, there was a guard, and we made a lot of noise. That is why I wanted to get out of there as fast as possible."

Aiden does not look at anyone as he says all of this. He just keeps his head straight and looks ahead at where he is going. I know he does not want to talk about what happened in there. It is too traumatic.

I want to say something to let him know that killing the guard does not make him a bad person, but I know he would not want anyone else to know unless he was comfortable with it. I have to let him talk about it when he is ready.

"Well, it sounds like they are getting creative. We will also have to get creative for when we go to the next town on the list. We need to be ready when they move the carnival to the next place. We should really try getting there before the carnival does. It would be nice if we could break into the town earlier to warn people and get them out," Theon says.

"Well, that sounds familiar," Devin says.

"Yeah, Theon, if you are the one warning people, then I don't think anyone is getting out," I say, remembering how he just yelled at me to get out of the carnival and did not explain anything else.

"I will work on it," Theon says while turning his head to glare at me.

"You are going to need to work hard, considering you kind of suck at it," I say with a little amusement in my voice.

We come up to the road that Aiden was talking about, and we follow it for a while before Aiden and Theon lead us off the smooth pavement and back into the woods. It does not take long until a small house that looks like it is falling apart comes into view, and I can see two people standing outside holding long sticks.

"Is that the camp?" Devin asks, sounding disappointed.

I try not to laugh while Theon turns around with a scowl on his face.

"No, that is not our camp. That is just a lookout to ensure no one finds us," Theon says.

One of the guys comes over to us, and I recognize him as Vesper.

"Well, that was faster than expected. Did you find the room I was talking about?" Vesper asks.

"Yeah, we found it," Aiden says, pulling out the notepad and map from his pocket. The map is folded up the same way it was before when I handed it to Aiden.

"I see you also found a gun," Vesper says, pointing to the gun that is strapped over Aiden's shoulder.

"I guess you could say that. We have two smaller guns as well. I have no idea how much ammo. I didn't check since I am not as good with guns as Balan, and I figured he should be the one to check it out," Aiden says.

"Well, speaking of Balan, he is waiting for you by the fire. He is waiting for everybody, actually," Vesper says. "I think he is excited to know we were able to get people out this time. All the injured are in the brown tent if anyone wants to say hello to them."

With that, Vesper returns to his spot on the deck of the small house, and we follow Aiden and Theon through the woods further until we come across their camp. Most of the camp has no coverage over it. There are a few small homemade tents, but they don't look well built. One storm or a powerful gust of wind could easily knock some of them down. A few fires are going on in various places, and most of the people I see are sitting or sleeping around them.

A few people look up at us in curiosity and I do not know what to do. Do I introduce myself and say hello? I ignore them and follow Aiden as he leads us further into the camp, where I see some food cooking over a larger fire and people lifting buckets of water and putting them into smaller containers.

There are people cutting wood with a saw and another group of people using string to tie things together. I do not know what they are making, but I am interested in their work.

A guy who looks to be in his forties comes up to us. "There you are. I was wondering when you would arrive," he says to Aiden. He then turns his body to face the rest of the group and introduces himself. "Hello, hello. I am Balan, and I was a police officer in Tundris. I would like to welcome you guys into our camp, and I would like to apologize for the things you have probably seen within the last twenty-four hours. We went through the same thing just two months ago," he says grimly.

"I would like to encourage you guys to stay and make yourselves comfortable. If you need anything, let me know. I will be happy to answer." Balan continues, "We do not have the best accommodations right now, but I will ensure you all have somewhere to sleep tonight."

Balan looks to Aiden, "As some of you may or may not know, this is my son Aiden, and I know he will also be happy to help you if you need anything."

Balan looks around at our group once more, and he seems to be thinking about something. He speaks again when it looks like he has decided on his thoughts. "Aiden, why don't you bring them to one of the fires to rest for a little while? I will come find you all once you have had some sleep, and we can discuss where to go from there."

"Let's go to the closest fire over here," Aiden said while leading us to one of the many fires to the left. "We have not finished building proper shelters for everyone yet, so some of us sleep and spend our time hanging out by the fires we make. We don't want to make too big of a fire that would draw a lot of attention, so we make multiple small ones, typically around a flat part of the woods."

"Do you guys not sleep in that house back there?" Devin asks.

"No, we found some tools in it, but it is mostly rotted out and falling apart, so we use it as a lookout post," Aiden says.

"What do we do now?" I can't help but ask.

"Right now, we rest. It has been a long night," Aiden says. "Balan will probably come back in a few hours to talk to you guys about joining the jumpers and going to the next town."

I nod my head in understanding, and I approach a tree near the fire. I sit down and rest my head against the trunk, but I can't seem to bring myself to fall asleep. I know I am tired, but it is like my body knows I am exposed here out in the woods and is refusing to let me sleep.

I look at the rest of the group and see that some of them are also struggling to sleep.

"Just close your eyes," Devin says. "You will fall asleep eventual-ly."

He sits beside me against the same tree, but his eyes are closed. I copy him by closing my own eyes and hoping that sleep will find me.

I don't know when I fell asleep, but I wake up when I feel something nudging my foot. When I open my eyes, I see Devin is the cause.

"Balan is back. Aiden says he wants to speak with everyone now." Devin says.

Looking around, I notice I am still against the same tree as before. The sky is still light, but it seems that a few hours have passed since I fell asleep.

More of our group from Treegrass are up and talking to one another around the fire, but most of their heads are turned towards the right, where Balan is standing.

"I know you all have had a rough night, and maybe some of you are not ready to answer me," I sit up straighter and hang onto every word he is saying, "but I would like to know who is interested in joining me and the Jumpers in our efforts to fight back against the New World. I would like to point out that you do not have to join the Jumpers. I do not want you to feel like you have to. We will take care of you regardless. I understand if you do not want to put your life at risk, but I just figured I would ask. You can join and back out at any time. You don't have to give me an answer right now. You can think about it for a while, but I just wanted to put that question out there." Balan says.

"As of right now, we are mostly focused on warning the other towns of what's to come. Hopefully, in the future, we can work our way up to taking back our homes and making sure no one else loses their lives due to the New World."

There is silence for a few seconds, and I look around to see if I can get a general idea of what people are thinking. From their faces, it seems like they have mixed emotions about joining the effort to fight the New World.

"I'm in," I say.

Devin looks at me in understanding, "You can count me in as well."

A few more people also want to get involved, but a significant number are still too afraid, and I understand why.

When no one else says anything, Balan speaks again, "We hold a meeting about once a week for everyone involved in the effort. These meetings are to share ideas and try to come up with our next move. We also try to have training every day at noon. Naturally, you guys have had a long night, so we can wait a few days before starting. We do not have many supplies, but we do our best to share what we have with everyone. There aren't really any permanent sleeping spots. We are working on that, but just try to make yourself at home for now."

Someone approaches Balan, and he excuses himself before leaving. The rest of our group looks around at the camp, and I can tell that none of us know what to do now.

Aiden comes over and sits by Devin and me.

"Why don't you rest some more? You still look tired," Aiden says to me. "I have let Balan know everything we had seen in there. Tomorrow, we will discuss about what to do about the New World and the carnivals."

"We are going to make them pay," I tell Aiden.

"Yes, just not today. Try to go back to sleep," Aiden says. His voice tells me how tired he is.

Aiden leans his back on a nearby tree and closes his eyes.

"He is right," Devin says. "We are both going to need our energy if we are going to go up against the New World."

I feel the exhaustion take over my body, and I close my eyes and try to relax, but Devin's words stick in my brain. We are both going up against the New World. I know he is strong, but I can't help but worry about losing him to them, just like my Mom and Dad.

I think about all the people the New World killed, and I think about all the ways I could get back at them. They can't get away with what they did.

I will not let them.

Epilogue

One month later:

Kaz throws a punch at me, and I block it with ease.

Balan has been teaching us the basics of fighting just in case we ever run into trouble with anyone from the New World. Balan wants us to be as prepared as possible for when we leave for Lewisville. He has been training us every day, just like he said he would. According to Aiden, Balan's training has gotten more vigorous since he told him all about our experience when we went back into the carnival.

The Jumpers do not feel safe when Balan is gone. He promised them from the start that he would stay behind to guard the camp in case the New World sent their shooters after them. Because of this, Balan wants everyone going to the other towns to be as prepared as possible.

Today, Kaz and I are working on hand-to-hand combat. This requires us to learn to throw a punch and block one as well.

I have gotten pretty good at avoiding being hit or kicked, but I need to work on my attack. Kaz is from Tundris and has been working with the Jumpers since they escaped their carnival. She has gotten pretty good at attacking and blocking, but I am faster than her.

I swing at her with my right arm. She leans back at the last second, and I miss her. I see her take a step forward to punch me, but I quickly move to the side, and the two of us end up circling each other, watching to see what the other will do.

"Keep your eye on your opponent. Remember to look at your opponent's eyes. Also, make sure you look at how their body moves," Balan says.

He always says things like this, but I don't fully understand. He tells us to look at their eyes and body at the same time. How is that possible? I only have one set of eyes.

"Learning your opponent's habits and tells are crucial to beating them," he says.

Balan was a police officer in Tundris, which means that he had to train in the town of Officials. Therefore, he knows the most about fighting. I do my best to listen to him and do what he says since he knows best, but I don't understand half of it.

Aiden helps me sometimes when I am not getting things, but he is out today with Vesper. Devin and Theon are just a short distance from me and Kaz. They are currently working on learning to disarm a person. Balan took the bullets out of the guns so that we could learn to take or knock a weapon out of our enemy's hands.

I am about to attempt to knock Kaz's feet out from under her when someone comes running up to us.

"They are on the move again," they say. "They are starting to pack up the carnival at Treegrass. At the rate they are going, they will be done and on the move within two days."

"Okay, everyone knows what to do," Balan states. "Pack what you need, be ready, be on the lookout, and get the people of Lewisville out of there. You will have to meet up with Aiden and Vesper on the way. Take the ATVs and follow the markings they left on the trees."

Aiden and Vesper have been trying to find Lewisville on their own by following the map we stole from the shooters. Using their knives, they have been marking certain trees so that we all know which way they went and we could follow them when the time came.

We were hoping to find Lewisville before the New World government was ready to send the carnival out again, but that is no longer an option. I guess we will have to catch up with them and hope we get to Lewisville before the carnival does.

I hope I will not have to use the things that Balan has taught us about fighting, but I think I am prepared if it comes to that. I feel ready. I feel confident. There are butterflies in my stomach that say otherwise, but I ignore them.

I look at Devin, silently asking him if he is ready, and he gives me a small nod.

"Let's go then," I tell him.

www.ingramcontent.com/pod-product-compliance
Lightning Source LLC
Chambersburg PA
CBHW070925190726
48292CB00004B/1104